'At least let's

'You may not lik
together, and we're not going to be able to do
that if you're on the defensive every time I'm
around. I only have to walk into the room and
I can feel the barriers come up.'

Frowning, Beth manoeuvred the small car
round the bend in the road. 'I'm sorry. I
wasn't aware that was what I was doing. It's
just that I'm trying to do my job and it isn't
easy, not when I'm constantly being made to
feel as if I'm on trial.'

'Is that really how you feel?' Sam looked
genuinely surprised. 'If so, I'm sorry. I'm not
the enemy, Beth,' he said quietly.

Jean Evans was born in Leicester and married shortly before her seventeenth birthday. She has two married daughters and several grandchildren. She gains valuable information and background for her Medical Romances™ from her husband, who is a senior nursing administrator. She now lives in Hampshire, close to the New Forest and within easy reach of the historic city of Winchester.

Recent titles by the same author:

THE DEVOTED FATHER
A LEAP IN THE DARK

MOTHER ON CALL

BY
JEAN EVANS

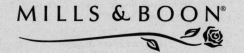

MILLS & BOON®

*All the characters in this book have no existence outside the imagination
of the author, and have no relation whatsoever to anyone bearing the
same name or names. They are not even distantly inspired by any
individual known or unknown to the author, and all the incidents are
pure invention.*

*First published in Great Britain 2002
Harlequin Mills & Boon Limited,
Eton House, 18-24 Paradise Road, Richmond, Surrey TW9 1SR*

© Jean Evans 2002

ISBN 0 263 83063 2

*Set in Times Roman 10½ on 12 pt.
03-0402-47795*

*Printed and bound in Spain
by Litografia Rosés, S.A., Barcelona*

CHAPTER ONE

'MUMMY! Mummy! Look at me. I'm jumping up to the sky.'

'Well done, Sophie.' Beth Jardine smiled and waved at her small, dungaree-clad daughter before exchanging ruefully amused glances with her mother. 'Where does she get her energy from? In this heat, too. It's turned out to be a real scorcher. Not exactly typical autumn weather, is it?'

'I know. Isn't it wonderful?' Anne Frazer used a programme sheet to fan her flushed cheeks. 'We couldn't have had a better day for the fair, could we? And to think, this morning it looked like rain.'

'Judging from the turnout, I should think there's a good chance they'll raise the extra funds they need.' Beth watched, smiling, as her father helped his grand-daughter to climb off the bouncy castle. 'What did you say it was in aid of?'

'The new community centre. I have to say, it's long overdue. The old village hall should have been demolished years ago. Ah, here's your father now.' Anne Frazer smiled. 'Perhaps now we'll get that drink at last. I don't know about you but I'm parched. I should think Sophie could do with a drink of something cool, too.'

'As soon as they come back we'll find you a nice cool patch of shade somewhere, and I'll head over to the refreshment tent. With any luck the rush will have died down by now. Sophie!' Grinning, Beth hoisted her daughter up into her arms, smoothing the sweat-dampened hair from Sophie's flushed cheeks. 'Did you enjoy yourself? Gosh, you're warm.'

'She's not the only one.' Paul Frazer used a hanky to mop at his forehead. He eased his shoulders and pressed a hand briefly to his chest, something Beth had seen him do earlier when he'd thought no one had been watching. It was on the tip of her tongue to ask him if he was all right when he suddenly headed off in the direction of some nearby trees.

'Come on. I spy a table and some benches. Let's all go and cool down in the shade then I'll go and get some drinks.'

'I'll do that, Dad,' Beth said. 'You sit down. You've been chasing after Sophie for the past half-hour. I'm not surprised you're tired.'

'I'm fine.' He turned to watch his granddaughter as she sat on the grass, picking daisies. But Beth wasn't entirely convinced.

A few weeks earlier her mother had written to say that he was feeling a bit under the weather. The symptoms she had described were all a bit vague—tiredness, dizziness, shortness of breath. 'Probably a touch of flu. Everyone's going down with it,' her mother had said. But Beth couldn't quite manage to stem a slight feeling of anxiety, especially as she watched him now.

It wasn't as if she could pin this feeling on anything specific. The fact that she was a doctor should have made her able to look at things with a professional eye, but that ability seemed to have deserted her just when she most needed it. He was her father and she loved him, and right now her instincts were working overtime where he was concerned.

Which made her all the more glad that she had decided to move to Cornwall to be close to her parents.

Living more than a hundred miles away, it had meant that she'd only seen them on a few occasions during the year, whenever she'd been able to fit it in with her work as a locum. But, hopefully, that was all behind her now—provided the job interview went well, of course.

She had no reason to suppose that it wouldn't. When she had briefly met the practice senior partner, Douglas Reynolds, he had seemed both friendly and welcoming, which had to be a good omen. Beth certainly hoped so, not only for herself but more especially for Sophie. And she knew her parents were thrilled at the prospect of being able to lavish their affection upon their only grandchild at last.

'Just look at the pair of them.' Anne sat down on the bench, from where she could watch them. 'They're having a whale of a time.' She smiled at Beth. 'I can't tell you how pleased we are that you decided to come and live in Pengarrick, Beth. It was awful, you being so far away and Sophie growing so fast. I know we saw you both at Easter for a couple of days, but children change so quickly, don't they?'

'Yes, they do.' Beth followed the direction of her mother's gaze and felt a strong tug of maternal pride as she watched her daughter's excited actions. The bright early October sun seemed to highlight the short burnished chestnut of her hair. 'I'm sure it was the right decision,' she said. 'I know I needed to be where the work was, but living in the centre of a busy town wasn't good for Sophie.'

'Well, she'll certainly get plenty of good fresh air down here, that's for sure. I know the cottage isn't exactly large...'

'It's fine for what we need.' Beth smiled. 'There's a

garden, too. Sophie's already decided that she'd like a swing and a rabbit.'

'It's good to see her looking so fit and happy. I still find it hard sometimes to believe she actually survived the accident. You'd never guess to look at her now that she spent all those weeks in hospital.'

'I suppose that's the one good thing about it,' Beth said quietly. 'She was too young to remember.'

'Still, all that's behind you now.' Anne injected a more positive note into her voice. 'What with the cottage and the new job...'

'I don't *have* the job yet, Mum.' Beth gave a rueful laugh. 'I met Dr Reynolds briefly when I came to take a look round the practice, but I still have to go for an interview. That's when I'll meet the other partners.'

'Yes, but I'm sure it's only a formality, dear.' Anne was blithely dismissive.

'I wish I had your confidence.'

'Your mum's right. You'll be fine.' Paul eased the neck of his T-shirt. 'You're a good doctor. They'd be fools to turn you down.'

'You don't think you may be just a shade biased, both of you?'

'Well, that's our privilege,' he said gruffly. 'You've been through a lot this past couple of years and still managed to come up smiling. In my book that takes a lot of courage.'

'Oh, Dad.' Beth swallowed hard on the sudden tightness in her throat. 'I couldn't have done it without you both.'

'Aye, well, I just wanted you to know. We're glad to have the pair of you where we can look after you for a change.'

'It's a nice thought, but I am twenty-nine, Dad.'

'Still a baby.' He grinned. 'You'll always be our baby, won't she, Annie? It's when you get to my age that you need to start worrying.'

Beth gave a slight laugh. 'Poor old things. Look, why don't you sit down and take a breather, and I'll go and find some nice cool drinks? Things look a bit quieter over by the refreshment tent now.'

Her confidence proved unfounded, however, but at least it was slightly cooler in the tent. Pushing back the tendrils of chestnut hair that had fallen against her warm cheek, she joined the queue and gazed round at the noisy crowds, all determinedly seeking refuge from the heat of the sun.

Beth smiled, thinking that it was an added bonus—like a holiday. She knew that even in the space of a few weeks her face had acquired a sprinkling of golden freckles, and her arms in the cap-sleeved T-shirt were faintly tanned. And it was wonderful to see Sophie looking so happy.

Beth sighed contentedly as she finally reached the counter and paid for the large, plastic cups of fizzy drinks. Yes, everything was going to be all right. For the first time in a long time she actually felt positive. The sun was shining. All was right with the world. What could possibly go wrong?

'Oh!' She stepped back and heard a kind of muffled grunt as her soft curves made contact with a hard, unyielding male body.

The man's hand closed round her waist, his palm in the small of her back, before things became confusing.

The shock of that heated contact sent her pulses leaping in frantic disorder and she moved jerkily, one hand flattening against his chest in her efforts to back away.

She stumbled, feeling the hard edge of a display unit

jabbing the small of her back, and a generous measure of the bright orange-coloured drinks spilled onto the floor.

She might have followed it but for the strong hands that grasped her firmly and hauled her upright once more.

'Careful, there. Are you OK?' The voice was deep and warm, distinctly male, and blue eyes quizzed her in a way that made her heart begin to thump.

Winded slightly, Beth struggled to gather in a breath and found herself focusing on a powerfully masculine physique that left her feeling decidedly shaky. Her legs were suddenly unaccountably weak and she became aware of a tingling warmth where his fingers had closed on her arms.

'I...I'm fine...I think. I'm not exactly sure what happened.' Her gaze shot upwards. It had a long way to go. Not short herself, he must have been well over six feet. Her eyes passed up the white T-shirt to the bronzed column of his throat before her eyes fastened with growing horror on the bright orange stain that was slowly spreading across his chest.

She gritted her teeth as embarrassment sent the colour scorching into her cheeks.

'Oh, no! Look, I'm so sorry.'

'Don't worry about it. It was probably my fault. You stepped back and I was standing too close,' he said. Still retaining his hold on her, he eased himself out of the queue, taking her with him.

'Perhaps I can do something... Wash it...' She broke off, conscious that she was being shrewdly assessed by eyes which were regarding her with a hint of amusement.

'Shall I relieve you, temporarily, of one of those?

Would that help?' He took one of the cups from her wavering hand. 'There isn't much room in here, is there?'

It was an odd feeling, being assessed in that way. It left Beth feeling uncomfortably breathless, though that could be put down to the collision, of course. It was shock, she told herself, and had absolutely nothing to do with the fact that his hand was still under her elbow.

'I thought the rush would have died down by now. I suppose it's the heat. Everyone wants cool drinks. It's probably just as well I wasn't carrying hot tea.' She paused momentarily, aware that she was babbling, and cast a swift glance over his lean, muscled length. 'I really am sorry if I did you any damage,' she added, though she suspected it would take rather more than a minor collision with an absent-minded female to make a dent in him.

Beneath the white T-shirt, his shoulders were unmistakably wide, his body tapering to a firm, narrow waist and long, jeans-clad legs.

'I think I'll survive.' His mouth made a brief dismissive twist that softened the hard-boned angularity of his features and did very strange things to her already overworked pulse rate. 'Shall we move to a slightly less crowded spot while you regain your breath?'

He led her towards the opening of the tent where a slight breeze certainly took some of the heat out of her cheeks. She set the plastic cups down on a nearby table and he handed her a tissue to wipe her hands. He had nice hair, she thought irrelevantly, short, dark, well styled, so that you could imagine running your fingers through it.

She drew herself up sharply. What on earth was she

thinking of? Embarrassed by the turn her mind had taken, she reached for one of the cups and took a long drink, tilting her head back as she swallowed, savouring its refreshing coolness.

His glance moved over her, taking in the calf-length slightly flared skirt which emphasised her slender waist, and shifting over her softly rounded figure before sliding down over the smooth shapeliness of her legs. His gaze lingered for a moment, making her skin heat in response, and she drew a swift, silent breath, confused by her reaction to a mere glance.

'I haven't seen you around before,' he said. 'Do you work locally?'

She shook her head. 'No, at least not yet. Actually, I'm in the process of finding a job.'

'What sort of work do you do?'

'I'm a doctor.'

'Really? So are you looking for something at the hospital?'

'No. I'm really more interested in general practice.'

'Why is that?'

She frowned briefly, slightly bemused by his obvious interest. 'Oh, I suppose because I enjoy the personal contact—getting to know the patients, rather than working in a hospital where you see so many different people and never really get to know them.'

'I can understand that. I take it you enjoy your work?'

'Oh, yes, very much.' She gave a wry smile. 'Or at least I will, if I get the job I've applied for. I moved to the area a few weeks ago. I managed to rent a small cottage and I've just about got things straight, so all I need now is the job. It would be nice to get settled into a proper routine again.'

'Yes, I imagine it would,' he murmured, smiling faintly. 'Weren't you taking a bit of a risk, moving to the area before you'd actually landed the job? Or perhaps you're confident you'll get it?'

'Not at all.' She gave a slight laugh.

'So what will you do if you're not successful?'

Beth frowned. 'I'm not sure. I haven't thought that far ahead. Find something else, I suppose. There were a number of reasons why it seemed a good time to move to Cornwall...'

'So, I take it you live fairly locally?'

A faint sense of caution began to stir in her. She didn't know this man from Adam, but she was beginning to sense that he wouldn't mind getting to know *her*. She hadn't missed the gleam of interest, but that didn't mean she was about to respond to it. There were more than enough uncertainties in her life at the moment.

All the same, she did owe him something, if only polite conversation, since she'd assaulted him, albeit unintentionally, and he'd been good enough not to make a fuss about it. So she said noncommittally, 'The cottage is quite close to the harbour. I think the owner decided to live abroad and I was lucky enough to come along at just the right moment when they decided to look for a tenant.'

The man shifted his position and she became aware of people trying to get by. Carefully she lifted the plastic cups and stepped to one side.

'I should go,' she said, conscious that she was being pushed closer to him as people tried to join the queue in search of refreshments. She was disturbingly aware of his long-limbed body. The way he was looking at her made her pulse accelerate in a heart-stopping way.

'That's a shame,' he said. 'Just as we were getting to know each other. I was thinking, perhaps we could meet up again…talk a little more…over a drink.'

'I…I'm really not sure that would be a good idea.' She hadn't been prepared for the impact this man had had on her. He was a stranger. She couldn't possibly be reacting to him the way she seemed to be.

'I'm only suggesting a drink,' he persisted, smiling at her. 'Nothing to be afraid of in that, is there?'

'I… No,' she said, shaken by the realisation that for a few seconds there she had almost wavered.

His dark brow lifted fractionally, and she took a deep breath. It had been a long day. She was hot and tired. Besides, there was Sophie to think of. What with one thing and another, things seemed to be getting rapidly out of hand. 'Look, I really can't,' she told him firmly. 'I'm sorry again about what happened, but now I must go.'

She was aware of his gaze narrowing on her, but she hurried away from him before he could delay her with more arguments. She sensed that he wasn't the kind of man who was used to being thwarted in any way, but that wasn't her problem, was it? Her parents were probably wondering what had happened to her.

Flustered, she gathered up the cups and began making her way through the crowds, taking care not to have another accident. She had only gone a few yards when she heard someone call after her.

'Wait.'

Her gaze swung round. It was the stranger. He was following her! She shook her head, determined not to be delayed any longer. It was late afternoon. Sophie would be tired by now. Time to get her home.

He called to her again as she sped across the grass,

ducking beneath overhanging trees in the hope of
throwing him off the scent. She couldn't believe he was
doing this. Didn't the man know the meaning of the
word 'no'?

He was gaining ground. Her heart was racing. She
hardly dared risk a look round, but she had to be sure.
Yes, he was still heading in her direction, his gaze
locking with hers, his hand raised, until his path was
blocked by a group of children.

He was certainly persistent, this man, and it made
her all the more determined to lose him. Yes, he was
attractive, and he'd seemed nice enough, but that was
no guarantee. He was far too persistent and that worried
her.

With a tiny gasp of relief she saw her parents and
Sophie in the shade of the trees where she had left
them.

Feeling hot and decidedly shaky, with an effort she
managed to force a smile. 'Here we are, then, cold
drinks all round.' Except that by now they were luke-
warm!

Anne smiled. 'You're looking very flushed, dear.'

Beth wiped the thin film of sweat from her forehead.
'Yes, it was fairly crowded in the tent.' And the fact
that she had practically run back hadn't helped! She
collapsed onto the bench. 'Here you go, Sophie. I
bought you a nice cool orange drink.'

'I don't want a drink. I want to play. Come on,
Grandad. Let's go on the slide.' Sophie was tired of
making daisy chains. She was on her feet, tugging im-
patiently at Paul's hand.

'Sophie, Grandad's tired.'

'It's all right, love, I'm fine. I'll keep an eye on her.
You sit down and take a breather, you look as if you

need it. Come on then, tiger.' They set off together.
'Mind how you go up those steps, Sophie.'

Beth shaded her eyes to watch the pair of them walk
off across the grass before sending a troubled glance
in her mother's direction. 'Mum, is Dad all right?'

'All right, dear?' Anne was suddenly investigating
the contents of her bag with far greater intensity than
it warranted.

'I know you said he hadn't been too well. You
thought it was a touch of flu.' Beth frowned. Her heart
was beginning to steady at last. 'He just doesn't seem
his usual self, that's all.' She turned her head to look
at her mother. 'I take it he has seen a doctor?'

'Yes, dear.'

'Recently?'

'Well, no, not exactly. He thought old Dr Benson
might give him a bottle of tonic or something, a bit of
a pick-me-up. You know?'

'And did he?'

Anne was unusually sombre.

'Mum, what is it?' Beth met her mother's troubled
gaze. 'What exactly did the doctor say?'

'Now, there's nothing for you to worry about.'

'Mum! I shall worry all the more if you don't tell
me.'

'Well, I don't completely understand it myself, but
he said your dad has…an irregular heartbeat. That's
why he's been feeling so tired lately apparently.'

Beth felt her own heart give a sudden jolt. 'And what
is the doctor doing about it?'

'Oh, he gave your dad some tablets to try.'

'Mum, why on earth didn't you tell me?'

'We didn't want to worry you, dear. There was nothing you could do and, anyway, Dad says he feels fine.

Of course, old Dr Benson retired fairly recently, and you know your dad. He hates change. He hates feeling *ill*.'

'I can understand that, Mum. But I do think it might be a good idea if he saw someone else—registered with a new doctor.'

'I'm sure you're right, dear.' Anne sighed. 'But you know how stubborn he is. Perhaps you can talk to him.'

Beth made up her mind she would do just that as soon as an opportunity arose. She smiled as her daughter came running towards her a few minutes later.

'Mummy, I'm hot.'

'I know, sweetheart. Look, have a nice cold drink and then I really think I should take you home. It's been a long, busy day.' She gathered the small figure up in her arms, hugging her. 'What you need is a nice cool bath, something to eat and then off to bed.'

She looked at her mother. 'You don't mind if we leave you, do you? Only I think this young lady has had quite enough excitement for one day.'

'No, of course not, love,' her father said. 'We'll be leaving fairly soon, too. Your mother just wants to pop over to see if there's anything left on the cake stall.'

'I'll phone you tomorrow, then?' Beth rose to her feet, holding her daughter by the hand. 'Come on, poppet. Let's go and find the car.' It had been standing in the car park in the sun all afternoon and was probably like an oven. Just as well she had thought to leave the windows cracked open, she thought as they began to make their way across the grass.

They were close to the car park when she saw the man she had met earlier in the refreshment tent bearing down upon them, and at the sight of him she almost froze in shock. She saw him raise his hand as if to attract her attention.

'Wait.'

'Come on, Sophie, let's hurry, shall we?'

'But I can't, Mummy. I'm tired.'

'Yes, I know, sweetheart, but we're nearly there. Look, there's the car, just over there.' She ushered Sophie towards the vehicle whilst fumbling in her pocket for her keys.

Beth dared to glance briefly over her shoulder. She couldn't believe he was still following her and, worse, gaining ground. Couldn't the man take no for an answer?

With shaking fingers she struggled to unlock the car door and virtually thrust Sophie inside, lifting her into her seat and snapping the seat belt into place.

She was about to launch herself into the driver's seat when he finally caught up with her.

'I've been trying to find you for the past couple of hours,' he said grimly. 'Dammit, you were running as if the devil was after you. I almost didn't catch you.'

Beth stared at the hard line of his mouth. 'What on earth are you doing?' she bit out, a note of panic edging her voice as she realised that he had actually admitted that he had been following her. Then a surge of annoyance took over. 'How dare you come after me?' she snapped. 'Are you out of your mind?'

A muscle flicked in his jaw. 'I had no choice. You took off like a bat out of hell.'

With good reason, obviously, she thought. 'Look,' she said tautly, 'I told you I didn't want to see you. I don't know you. I don't *want* to know you. I thought I'd made that perfectly clear.'

Beth deliberately kept her voice low so that Sophie

wouldn't hear. 'Just go away and stop pestering me,' she hissed.

'I can't until I've—'

It was too much. He was still determined to pester her. Beth's temper erupted. Hurling herself into the car, she dragged the door to, but not before she'd seen it catch his elbow with a glancing blow.

His harsh grunt of pain made her wince, and for a second or two her hold on the door weakened as she saw him pale. Briefly he closed his eyes, clutching at his injured arm. It was clear that she'd done him some damage.

Clenching his teeth, he withdrew his hand, and she hesitated only for a second before instinct took over. She couldn't afford to offer sympathy. She had Sophie to think of.

'Go away and leave me alone,' she said again. 'If you don't I'll scream for help.' Then she slammed the door properly shut and locked it.

She was desperately trying to insert the key in the ignition when he began tugging at the window. He wasn't going away and now he was really angry. With a slight sob she turned the key and almost wept as the engine sprang into life. Then she gasped as he pushed something through the slight gap at the top of the window.

It fell onto her lap. She stared at it in growing dismay. 'Oh, no,' she whispered as comprehension slowly dawned. 'Oh, no…what have I done?' It was her purse. She hadn't even noticed it was missing until now. She closed her eyes briefly. Oh, Lord, what had she done? She'd assumed the man had been following her in order to make a nuisance of himself, when all the time…

Her heart racing, she switched off the engine and

slowly opened the door. He had moved away and was leaning against another car, nursing his injured arm.

Tentatively, she called out to him. 'Wait, please. I think…I think I may have made a terrible mistake.'

'Oh, really?' he snarled through gritted teeth. 'I wonder how that could have happened?' His tone was full of dry sarcasm, and she bit nervously at her lower lip before holding up the purse.

'I owe you an apology,' Beth said humbly. 'I hadn't realised I'd lost it.'

'I found it just after you left the tent. You must have dropped it. Perhaps you'd better check the contents,' he tossed back coldly. 'I wouldn't want to be accused of misappropriating anything simply as an excuse to get to know you better.' The iciness of his tone chilled her to the bone, leaving her feeling more guilty than ever. His mouth was set in a grim line, and she didn't think it was entirely because of the pain she had inflicted.

'Look, I really don't know what to say. I had no idea. I thought—'

'Lady, I *know* what you thought,' he cut in with knife-like precision. 'Just check the contents and I'll be on my way.'

'I'm sure I don't need to. Look, I feel awful about this. Will you at least let me take a look at your arm? Is it very painful?' Unthinkingly she reached out a hand.

He recoiled. 'Save it.' He nursed his injured arm. 'All I can say is I feel sorry for your patients, and you won't be surprised to hear I've had enough for one day.'

Beth swallowed hard. 'Please, let me do something to make amends,' she said. 'I have a first-aid box in the car.' She reached into the glove compartment. 'I can probably fix up a sling for you.'

'I don't think so. I have to drive.'

She pressed her lips together as she looked at his arm. 'The skin is slightly broken, and I'm afraid you're going to have a nasty bruise.'

'I'll live.' He was silent as she cleaned the injury, and as she applied an antiseptic cream she murmured diffidently, 'When you called after me, you were just trying to tell me that you'd found my wallet, weren't you? I thought—'

'You thought I was lusting after your body,' he cut in. 'You flatter yourself.'

She had deserved that, but it stung all the same. 'I think your arm will be all right,' she said. 'I'm sure nothing's broken, but you might want to take a couple of painkillers when you get home. Will you be able to drive?'

'I'll manage.' He glanced at her handiwork. 'At least I can't fault your first-aid skills.'

She flinched at the sarcasm. 'I'm really very sorry,' she said again.

His mouth moved in a parody of a smile, and there was an ice-cool glitter in his dark eyes as he said, 'I'll be on my way. I won't say goodbye because I dare say I shall see you around.' Then he walked away, leaving her to mull over his words.

There was something about them that took her aback. Somehow it hadn't sounded like a casual dismissal, and her heart contracted in a strange way as she watched him go. It was very unlikely they would ever meet again, surely? But the thought did nothing to ease her uncertainty. There was something about the way he had said it, almost as if it were a threat—or maybe a promise—and she wasn't at all sure she was happy with either.

CHAPTER TWO

'YOU'RE sure you don't mind looking after Sophie for me for a couple of hours?' Beth followed her mother into the kitchen.

'Mind! No, of course not. We've been looking forward to it. We're going to make some biscuits aren't we?' Smiling at her granddaughter, Anne Frazer helped Sophie out of her jacket before reaching for a smaller version of her own apron from the hook. 'You just relax, dear,' she told Beth. 'We'll be fine. You concentrate on your interview.'

Beth groaned. 'I'll be glad when it's over.'

'Today's the day, then, pet?' Beth's father came to join them in the kitchen, depositing a basket of fresh vegetables on the table.

Beth managed a smile. 'I was just saying to Mum that I'll be glad when it's over and I know one way or the other.' Glancing at her watch, she headed for the door. 'I'd better go or I'll be late, and that wouldn't look too good, would it? Cross fingers for me.'

'We'll have the champagne on ice ready to celebrate.'

Paul's voice was faintly distracted and Beth looked at him as he pulled out a chair and sat down. He looked pale and tired.

'Dad, are you feeling all right?'

'I'm fine. Just a bit breathless after digging the carrots, that's all.'

She frowned. 'Look, I know old Dr Benson died, but

don't you think you should register with someone else and ask for an appointment to see the specialist again?' Beth urged. 'It's been a while since they did the tests.'

'I'm fine, love. Besides, I can't go rushing off to the doctor every time I get a bit puffed, now, can I? They've far better things to do than keep seeing me.'

'That's what they're there for, Dad. It's their job.'

'Aye, well, I never did like taking tablets anyway, and I can't stand hospitals. I'm just getting older and when you get older you expect to have a few aches and pains every now and again.'

Anne Frazer raised an eyebrow. 'You're wasting your time. He won't listen. Stubborn as a mule, that's his trouble.'

Beth wasn't so easily put off. 'You're not old, Dad. You've got a lot of years ahead of you and there's absolutely no reason why you should put up with aches and pains. At least see a doctor again and ask him if he'll refer you to the specialist.'

'I really don't see the need. I'll think about it.'

Beth glanced at her mother, who shrugged help-lessly.

'I thought you had an interview to go to. You want the job, don't you?' Paul glanced at his daughter. 'Better not be late, then.'

Beth could see there was no point in pursuing the subject further at that moment. 'Right, well, wish me luck.'

'You don't need it. They'd be crazy to turn you down.'

Beth wished she had her parents' confidence. She was sure of her ability to do the job and she had liked what she had seen of The Gables Health Centre when she had paid a brief familiarisation visit a couple of months earlier. Douglas Reynolds, the senior partner, had gone out of his way to make her feel comfortable, introducing her to some of the staff who worked in the practice. She had been impressed by the friendly atmosphere. It was the sort of place where she would love to work.

Her hands tightened briefly on the steering-wheel as she drove along the coast road. So much depended on getting this job. Maybe that was why she felt so nervous. It all seemed so perfect—almost too perfect. The cottage she had managed to rent for herself and Sophie wasn't more than a mile from the surgery and the hours that had been specified would suit her perfectly. It *had* to work out, Beth thought. It just had to.

Manoeuvring carefully through the pretty village, she was pleased to see that her initial impression of the health centre had been right. The Gables was a fairly new single-storey building, with plenty of windows. Shrubs and tubs of flowers made a pleasing approach as she entered the car park and finally switched off the engine.

'Well, here goes.' Taking a few deep breaths, Beth climbed out, locked the car door and headed for the automatic doors leading into Reception.

'Hello, there. Can I help you?' A tall, slim, dark-haired girl came out of the office and smiled at Beth. 'I'm afraid the surgery is closed except for emergencies, but I can make an appointment for you...'

'Oh, no, I don't...' Beth gave a crooked smile. 'I'm Dr Jardine. Beth Jardine. I have an appointment with Dr Reynolds.'

'Dr Jardine! Yes, of course, we've been expecting you. Sorry I didn't recognise you. I think it was my day off when you visited the practice. Anyway, hi! I'm

Debbie Watson, practice manager. It's good to meet you at last.'

'Hello.' Beth took an instant liking to the girl. 'I think I may be a little early. I wasn't sure what the traffic would be like so I allowed myself plenty of time.'

'You're lucky it wasn't market day.' Debbie said wryly. 'You can't move. It's just as well it's only one day a week. Look, why don't you come through to the waiting room? I'll let Dr Reynolds know you're here.'

'I really don't mind waiting…'

'It's no problem.' Debbie gathered a folder from the reception desk. 'His last patient left about five minutes ago. I need him to sign these letters anyway.' She led the way through to the waiting room. 'Make yourself comfortable. I won't be long.'

She hurried away, leaving Beth to glance round the room. It was light and airy. A small coffee-table held an assortment of magazines. Beth picked one up and flicked through the pages but her stomach was churning too much to allow her to concentrate. Seconds later the door opened.

'Dr Jardine—Beth, my dear. It's good to see you again.' Douglas Reynolds took her hand in his and gave it a welcoming shake. He was a tall man of slim build, with brown hair greying at the temples, and his brown eyes held a friendly sparkle.

Beth guessed him to be somewhere in his early sixties and he was still a handsome-looking man. She had taken an instant liking to him at their first brief meeting, recognising the inherent warmth and compassion that seemed to emanate from him, and that feeling was reinforced again now.

'So, how are you?'

She gave a wry smile. 'A little nervous.'

'Oh, surely not.' He patted her hand and chuckled. 'Well, I promise we don't bite. Look, come on through to the office.' He led her through Reception. 'You remember Maggie, don't you?'

'Yes. Hello again.'

'Hi.' Maggie Pierce, The Gables' receptionist, replaced the phone after a call and quickly scribbled a note in the appointments diary as she glanced up and grinned. 'Nice to see you again. At least we're not quite so rushed off our feet this time. Perhaps I'll see you later?'

'Yes, I hope so.' Depending on whether or not she actually got the job, Beth thought.

'Perhaps you'd like a few minutes to freshen up?' Doug suggested.

She smiled, grateful to him for his thoughtfulness. 'Thank you. If you're sure I won't be taking up your valuable time?'

'There's no rush, my dear. My colleague, Dr Armstrong, is seeing his last patient now. He should be finished shortly. Of course, you haven't met him yet, have you?'

'No. I think he was away on a refresher course when I came for my preliminary visit.'

'Yes, that's right. He's looking forward to meeting you.' Doug Reynolds smiled. 'Would you like a cup of coffee? There's a Thermos jug ready in my office if you'd like to come through as soon as you're ready. The washroom is just down the corridor and to the right.'

Beth hurried to the room, where she quickly removed her coat and rinsed her hands. For a few sec-

onds, as she stared at her reflection in the mirror, she
was aware of a fluttering of nerves in her stomach.

It was tension, she reasoned. A natural reaction in
the circumstances. A lot depended on her getting this
job and although Doug Reynolds had assured her that
the interview would be strictly informal, she could still
feel the rush of adrenalin and knew she wouldn't settle
until it was all over, one way or the other.

Lightly running a comb through the heavy swathe of
her chestnut hair, she fervently hoped that her would-
be future employers would find nothing amiss with her
appearance. She was wearing a lightweight suit in
cream linen. Beneath the jacket she had on a terracotta
silk shirt. Was the skirt perhaps just a shade too short?
Well, if it was, it was too late to do anything about it.
Quickly touching up her make-up, satisfied that she
could do no more to make herself look presentable she
headed for the office.

'Do come in, my dear,' Doug said. 'So, tell me, how
do you like Pengarrick so far? I think you said you're
renting a cottage not too far from here?'

'Yes, that's right. I'm still finding my way around
but it's a beautiful area, isn't it? Especially down by
the harbour.' She smiled. 'I still can't get used to the
idea of drawing back the curtains in the morning and
looking out at the sea. It's so different to what we've
been used to.'

'Mmm, I know what you mean. I was a townie myself once. Couldn't go back to it now.'

'I can understand why.'

'Ah, and here's Sam now. Sam, come and meet Dr
Jardine. She's hoping to join us at The Gables. Beth—
Sam Armstrong. Sam—Beth Jardine.'

She turned, holding out her hand, and felt her heart

give a small painful jolt, the welcoming smile fading from her lips. She felt a sudden sinking sensation in the region of her stomach as she stared at the man advancing towards her.

She had expected to meet a stranger. Instead, his tall, lean frame was all too heart-sinkingly familiar, even as she told herself it wasn't possible, those rugged features were ones she had seen all too recently.

'You!' She groaned softly.

The dark blue gaze met hers and she felt a tide of warm colour surge into her cheeks.

'It's a pity you weren't here when Beth came for her visit,' Doug was saying. 'Still, I'm sure you'll soon get to know each other as we chat.'

'We've already met.' He appraised her coolly as his hand closed over hers. Instinctively she tried to pull away. The shock waves from that firm touch sent an odd jumble of signals through her nerve-endings and her insides gave an uneasy little quiver.

'You have?' Doug was clearly surprised.

'Yes. You could say we bumped into one another. Isn't that right?'

Glancing up quickly, Beth found herself staring into the thickly lashed, disturbingly blue eyes which, at that moment, were filled with sardonic amusement. His hand shifted briefly to his elbow and her own grey eyes flashed with annoyance.

This was awful. The job was as good as lost even before she got to the interview. She might just as well pack up now and go home. His mouth twisted as if he had read her thoughts.

'Quite a coincidence.' Doug gathered up some papers.

'Yes, isn't it?' Sam met Beth's gaze and she moistened her dry lips with her tongue.

Even if she got the job, would she really be able to work with this man when it was pretty obvious that he had already formed his opinion of her? As far as he was concerned, she was a hysterical female, not to be taken seriously.

'Well, I suppose we'd better get started. No point prolonging the agony, is there?' Doug smiled. 'Though I'm sure you'll find we're all quite friendly.'

Some more than others. Beth couldn't help the thought as she determinedly smiled a response.

'Would you like coffee before we start?'

She would have loved one, but she refused politely. With Sam Armstrong watching her every move, she couldn't be sure her hands wouldn't shake and she wasn't about to give him the satisfaction of seeing that she was in the least bothered by him. Too much depended on this job and if she was going to change his opinion of her, she needed to keep all her wits about her.

'In that case, come through to the staff room.' Doug led the way. 'I thought you'd find it less formal in here than the office. Take a seat, my dear. Make yourself comfortable.' He waved her towards a leather chair.

She sat, aware that Sam Armstrong remained standing over by the window.

'Right, well, let's make a start, then, shall we? I imagine you must be wondering why we need to take on another partner?'

Beth smiled. 'Yes, I must admit, the thought had occurred to me.'

'The fact is that I'm thinking of retiring in the not-too-distant future. My wife and I have decided we'd

like to see more of our family who are out in Australia.
Who knows? We may decide we like the place enough
to settle there ourselves. Anyway, Sam will obviously
take over here as senior partner, and it seemed sensible
to bring in a replacement now in order that whoever
gets the job will have time to get to know our system
of working—and the patients, of course.'

Beth smiled. 'I can see the logic in that.'

'I'm afraid we have very little in the way of excitement here in Pengarrick, Dr Jardine.' Sam Armstrong
spoke quietly from where he stood at the window.
'This is a relatively quiet community, with a prepon-
derance of elderly people. Don't you think you might
find it a little too quiet? Why would you want to leave
a large city to come and work in a small seaside town?'

'I'm not looking for excitement.' Beth turned her
head to look at him and felt her throat tighten for a
few seconds as his shrewd eyes met hers. 'And from
what I've seen of it, Pengarrick seems to be a nice,
healthy place in which to live and work. Plenty of
schools, shops, clean air. And as I've already explained
to Dr Reynolds, my parents live locally. It would suit
me to be close to them.'

'I'm sure it would.' He gave her a level look. 'The
question is, would it suit us? I'm sure you'll appreciate
that patients need a degree of security and…stability.'
Had she imagined it or had he emphasised the word?
'Someone who'll have the best interests of this practice
at heart. In other words, what guarantees can you offer
that we would be making the right choice in selecting
you?'

Beth moistened her dry lips with her tongue, studying his strong, angular features for some clue as to why
he was so determined to give her a hard time. Yes, it

was true, they hadn't exactly met on the best of terms, but she had hoped he might have put that behind him.

He was in his early thirties, she judged, and she guessed he must have considerable drive and self-motivation to be able to consider assuming responsibility for his own practice.

From what she had seen so far, Sam appeared to be aggressively masculine, and she couldn't imagine him veering off course in any way. Perhaps he didn't credit her with the same amount of stamina or staying power.

She said carefully, 'I hope I've always given both of those things. I'm not afraid of hard work and I've always enjoyed a good working relationship, both with colleagues and patients. I really don't foresee any problems.'

He moved towards the desk and glanced at her application form. 'I see you've been working as a locum for the past two years. Isn't that a little unusual?' He gave her a level look. 'It doesn't exactly fit in with your stated desire to offer a long-term commitment. Perhaps you'd care to explain what prompted your decision?'

A momentary bleakness came into Beth's eyes. She cleared her throat.

'Would you care to elaborate?' Doug Reynolds said gently. He glanced up from the notes he had been making to meet her gaze.

'I… Yes. My daughter, Sophie… She was involved in an accident a couple of years ago and had to spend some time in hospital. That's why I chose to do locum work. It meant I could spend more time with her, especially in the beginning. I had to be on hand when she needed me.'

Sam's gaze narrowed. 'I hadn't realised you were married.'

'You didn't ask.' She lifted a finely arched brow. 'I hadn't realised it was relevant.'

'It isn't,' Doug Reynolds smiled. 'But I'm sure you'll appreciate that any background information will help us to build up a picture. It's important for you as well as for us that the person we select will fit in—feel happy here.'

'Yes. Yes, of course.' Beth drew a deep breath and, with an effort, forced a smile. 'Dr Armstrong, I'm sure if you look at my references, you'll see that there was never any problem as far as my work was concerned. I was totally committed and, as I said, I'm not afraid of hard work.'

He flashed her a quick, appraising look, then nodded. 'I'm not questioning your references,' he said, more gently this time. 'If there were any doubts you wouldn't be here now.' He glanced down at the form once more, before adding, 'I take it your daughter has made a full recovery? I have to ask because, while the hours we're offering may seem convenient to you now, there may be times—staff holidays or sickness, for instance—when extra help is needed. How would that fit in with your plans? I take it you have some sort of care arrangements in place to ensure that you'll be able to concentrate fully on your work?'

'Yes, of course,' she said huskily. 'It's been a long, slow process, but Sophie is fine now. I'm hoping that the move will help her to regain confidence. That's why it's so important.'

He was obviously waiting for her to say more, but she stayed silent, warding off the painful memories that crowded into her head. She didn't want to speak about what had happened. Her feelings were still raw and she didn't want to risk opening up the wounds in front of him.

She looked down at her fingers, clenching and unclenching them. She stilled them quickly, smoothing her palms against the fabric of her skirt. 'I can assure you, it won't be a problem.'

'You moved to Pengarrick fairly recently,' Doug Reynolds said.

She smiled, sensing that she was on safer ground. 'I wanted to be closer to my parents. My father hasn't been too well recently. I felt my mother needed some moral support and, of course, it means they see more of Sophie.'

Sam Armstrong's eyes raked her slender figure, flicking over what he could see of her feminine curves which were outlined by the silk blouse she was wearing beneath her jacket, and then skimmed back upwards to rest on the oval of her face. Annoyingly she felt a rush of colour invade her cheeks.

'You're very young,' he said on a faint sigh. 'You look as though you've just come straight out of medical school.'

'I'm twenty-nine, Doctor. I can't help it if I look younger than I am. I can only repeat that I'm prepared to work hard, and I would certainly do my very best for the practice.'

'You'd have to, if you expect to stay. We can't afford to carry passengers.'

The brusque response scraped a raw edge along her nerves. Admittedly they hadn't got off to the best of starts but surely that didn't justify his antagonism towards her?

The older man intervened. He rose to his feet. 'Well,

I think we've asked all the questions we need to, Beth,'
he said. 'I'd just like a few minutes to speak with Dr
Armstrong. I'll get Maggie to show you around. You
might like to take a look at our computer system and
I'm sure she'll be able to answer any questions you
might have. We'll see you again shortly, by which time
we'll be able to let you know our decision.'

As if I didn't know it already, Beth thought as she
made her way out. She did her best to stifle a feeling
of disappointment. She had really wanted this job. It
would have offered the fresh start she and Sophie both
so badly needed. But there was no point dwelling on
it. There were formalities to be gone through, but it
wasn't going to happen and that was all there was to
it.

After a short tour of the practice with Maggie, she
sat down again outside the staff room.

'Dr Jardine?'

'What? Oh, yes.' Frowning, she turned to see Sam
standing in the doorway.

'We're ready for you now. If you'd like to come
back to the staff room.'

She glanced at him and wished she knew what he
was thinking, but his expression gave nothing away—
which she took as an ominous sign so that she was
stunned when Doug Reynolds smiled affably as she
entered the room and said, 'Well, my dear, let me put
your out of your misery. We'd like to offer you the
job, if you still want it, that is. We're more than happy
with your references, and the fact that you live so close
to the surgery has to be a big plus for us. So, what do
you say?'

She gave a short laugh. 'I...I'm absolutely delighted.' She was aware of Sam's glittering gaze on her.

'Good. That's settled, then. We look forward to having you as part of the team. I think you'll find we're a friendly crowd. Quite easy to work with, once you get to know us. Of course, you haven't met John yet, have you? He's taking a few days off. But he'll be here when you join us. I'm sure you'll get along splendidly.'

Doug smiled as he gathered up his papers and dropped them into his briefcase, and Beth couldn't help glancing in Sam's direction.

The merest flicker of a smile crossed his mouth as though he'd read her uneasy thoughts, but he said nothing, instead reaching for his jacket which was draped over the back of his chair.

Beth focused for a few seconds on his tanned throat, then she looked quickly away. Doug said, 'When do you think you'll be able to start? Obviously the sooner the better as far as we're concerned.'

Her mind raced. 'I should think by next week, if that's all right. Sophie will be starting at her new school then, so it will all tie in very nicely. Does that suit you?'

'Couldn't be better.' Doug reached for his diary and mobile phone. 'What about your husband? You didn't say what line of work he's in. Has he managed to find a job locally?'

'My husband died just over two years ago,' Beth told him, aware of Sam moving away from the window where he had been staring out at the traffic.

'My dear, I'm sorry to hear that. Things can't have been easy for you, especially bringing up a small child alone.'

Beth smiled faintly at Doug. 'We've coped. I've

been lucky. My parents have been wonderfully supportive, and they're more than happy to have Sophie during the school holidays while I'm at work. My mum's neighbour has a little girl the same age as Sophie. They get on well together and she's agreed to look after Sophie whenever my parents can't manage it.'

'Good. That must make life a little easier.' Doug glanced at his watch. 'Look, I'm sorry to cut and run but I promised to visit an elderly patient who's due to go into hospital tomorrow. He's feeling rather nervous and I want to try and put his mind at rest.' He was already heading for the door. 'Welcome again to the practice, my dear. We'll have a longer chat next week.'

The door closed behind him and she turned to meet Sam's cool, measured glance. For some reason she recalled his ominous words from their previous meeting.

She took a deep breath and said accusingly, 'You knew, didn't you, that we'd meet again?'

His mouth twisted wryly. 'It seemed a pretty safe bet. There's only one other medical practice in this area, and old Doc Walker is retiring in a couple of months. His son is taking over, and I know he's not looking for a new partner—not yet anyway.'

Her grey eyes glittered angrily. 'So why did you put me through this...this performance? Or was it just some sadistic whim? A chance to pay me back?'

'I don't know what you mean.'

'Oh, come on. You said—and I quote, "I feel sorry for your patients."'

'Yes, well, it *was* said in the heat of the moment. Extreme pain can have that effect.'

She expelled a harsh breath. 'It's pretty clear you don't really want me to have this job. Why didn't you just come out and say so?' Her lips tightened. 'This isn't going to work, is it?'

'I'd say that's up to you. My one concern is for Doug. He's had his heart set on retiring for the past six months.'

'But surely he isn't old enough to be thinking of retiring?'

'He's sixty-two. I agree, he could go on for years yet, but his wife, Rosemary, has multiple sclerosis. She's in remission at the moment, but they both know it can't last so Doug is anxious that they spend some quality time together, doing the things they'd always planned—starting with a holiday abroad, somewhere warm, and obviously he'll go with an easier mind if he knows that things are running smoothly here.'

Beth nodded. 'I can understand that.'

'So I'm sure you'll also understand that he needs— we *both* need—to be sure that whoever joins the practice will be the right person. Someone who intends to stay and give a hundred per cent commitment.'

'I've said I'm prepared to do that.'

'Doug's right, your references are excellent. Maybe I just caught you on a bad day.' Her lips parted on a protest but he continued as if he was unaware of it. 'We got off to a bad start, but we're both adults. I'm sure we can find some way to work together. Unless that's a problem for you?'

'No, I—'

It was almost a relief when Maggie Pierce tapped at the door and popped her head round. 'Oh, Sam, I'm glad I caught you. Can you come? There's been an accident outside the surgery. Old Mrs Burrows collided with a cyclist.'

'I'm on my way.' He was already reaching for his

briefcase and heading for the door. 'Can you get hold of Doug? We may need him. Alice Burrows is eighty if she's a day.'

'Oh, heavens. No, sorry, he left about five minutes ago.'

'Damn!'

Beth glanced at him quickly. 'Look, can't I help? It's what I'm here for after all. I have to start somewhere.'

Sam sent Beth a quick glance, his eyes dark, tension showing in the taut lines round his mouth, and she suspected he didn't willingly delegate. She said carefully, 'There's always a danger of fractures in the elderly. The sooner she's seen, the better.'

'Yes, you're right. Thanks.' He looked at Maggie as he hurried through Reception. 'Get her notes out for me, will you? Oh, and better check that the treatment room is clear.'

'Will do.' Maggie sped away.

It was raining and the pavement was slippery with damp leaves as they hurried out to where a small crowd had already gathered.

A bicycle lay in the road, its front wheel buckled. Beside it a young teenager sat, a hand clasped to his temple as a trickle of blood dripped gently down his face. He looked pale and close to tears.

Beth went straight to the frail-looking woman who lay on the pavement, leaving Sam to tend to the youngster.

'Hello, there. It's Mrs Burrows, isn't it? I'm Dr Jardine. Are you badly hurt?'

The woman's face twisted with pain, and for a moment or two she lay with a hand clutched to her chest, breathing deeply. 'It's my arm,' she managed at last.

'I fell. I didn't see the bike coming. It was all my fault,' she said tearfully, glancing at the boy. 'I stepped into the road. I just didn't see him... He's not badly hurt, is he?'

'No, I don't think so. Just a few scratches and bruises.' Beth smiled reassuringly. 'Dr Armstrong is taking a look at him now. Look, if I help you, do you think you can manage to sit up so that I can take a look at your arm and just check you over? Do you hurt anywhere else?'

Alice Burrows thought about it and shook her head. 'No, I don't think so. I must have flung my arm out as I fell.' Her mouth twisted. 'It all happened so quickly. I feel so silly.' The white-faced pensioner took a deep breath. 'All these people standing, watching.'

'Don't take any notice of them. They're just concerned.' Kneeling beside the woman, Beth very gently held the injured arm, carefully moving it, trying not to cause any more discomfort. She watched the woman's face for any sign of pain.

'You're lucky,' she said at last. 'Nothing's broken, but I think you may have sprained your wrist. Look, if I help, do you think you can stand? I'm sure you'd be much more comfortable and warmer if we can get you in to the surgery.'

'I...I don't know. I'll try.'

Beth glanced at Sam. 'How are you doing?' she asked softly.

'Nothing too serious here. Minor lacerations. Looks worse than it is. Scalp wounds always bleed profusely. How about your patient?'

'Possible sprained wrist. I've checked her over as best I can. I'm pretty sure there's nothing more serious. We're going inside, out of this rain.'

'Good idea. Debbie will take her to the hospital for X-rays if necessary. You take the treatment room. I'll use my room.'

Beth helped Alice slowly to her feet, supporting her gently with an arm around her waist. 'Lean on me. We'll take it very slowly. That's right. Nice and easy. No hurry.'

'You're very kind. I'm sorry to be so much trouble.'

'It's not any trouble at all. Here we are. This way.' Beth glanced, smiling, at Maggie who met them in Reception and led the way towards the treatment room. 'If you sit down… There, I'm sure that's more comfortable. Now, let's take another look at you, just to be on the safe side.'

She made another gentle examination.

'Ouch!'

Beth smiled sympathetically. 'I'm sorry. You're going to have a bruised knee, I'm afraid, but I don't think there's any serious damage. We'll get your arm cleaned up a bit. I'll try not to hurt you but I just need to get some of the dirt out of this graze. Then I'll put your arm in a temporary sling to make you more comfortable, and we'll send you to the hospital to get it X-rayed.'

'Oh, dear—do I have to?'

'Yes, I really think it would be best.' Beth said reassuringly. 'I'm pretty sure you've sprained your wrist, but we need to be sure there aren't any tiny fractures. There.' Using a swab, she gently cleaned the area. 'That looks better, doesn't it?'

'You've been very kind,' the elderly woman said tearfully. 'How's the young lad, do you know? I hope he's going to be all right. It was all my fault. If I hadn't stepped out…'

Beth held the woman's uninjured hand in hers. 'Now, you're not to worry about it. I've had a brief word with my colleague, Dr Armstrong, and he said there were just a few minor cuts. He's going to be fine.' She looked at her watch. 'You may know Debbie, our practice manager. She's volunteered to drive you to the hospital where they'll X-ray your arm and wrist, and make you more comfortable.'

'I'm being such a nuisance.'

'Nonsense. Accidents happen.' Don't they just? Beth thought. She knew all about accidents, and then some. 'Ah. Here's Debbie.'

Minutes later, having seen her patient out, Beth made her way along the corridor to Sam's consulting room. The door was ajar. She tapped and entered.

Sam glanced up. 'Hi. How's the patient?'

'On her way to hospital—purely as a precautionary measure,' she added quickly, seeing the sudden look of concern on the youngster's face.

'She is going to be all right, isn't she? It all happened so fast. I was riding along and suddenly she just stepped into the road. I couldn't avoid her.'

'I know. Mrs Burrows explained,' Beth said reassuringly.

'No serious damage then?' Sam deftly applied a Steri-strip to the cleaned head wound.

'No. A sprained wrist. I thought it best to get it X-rayed, just to be on the safe side.'

He nodded. 'We're just about finished here. Young Daniel's got a few cuts and bruises. There we are— last one. That should do the trick.' He stood back to view his handiwork. 'Right, young man, that's you sorted.'

Daniel slid down from the couch. He gently probed the wound on his forehead and winced.

'A couple of paracetamol should help to get rid of the headache,' Sam advised. 'Don't play football for a few days. Try to keep the cut clean. I'm sure you'll be fine, but if you're at all worried, come back and see me.'

He watched as his patient left. 'Ah, well, two satisfied customers.'

'Alice was lucky. Patients of her age so often end up with a broken hip after a fall like that.'

'Oh, Alice is a tough old bird.' Sam scrubbed his hands and dried them. 'She lives on her own.'

'Doesn't she have a family?'

'Two sons, three daughters and heaven knows how many grandchildren—all living locally.'

Beth stared at him. 'Don't they care?'

'Of course they do. They all but came to blows when Alice's husband died about five years ago, trying to decide who should have Alice to live with them. They might have saved themselves the trouble. Alice wasn't having any of it. She told them in no uncertain terms that she was perfectly happy where she was, thank you very much. So she still lives in the cottage she moved into when she and Donald married fifty years ago. I pop in from time to time, just to keep an eye on her, and she sees the family when it suits her.'

'Sounds like a good arrangement to me.'

'Absolutely. I'm all for pensioner power.' Sam reached for his jacket, shrugging himself into it. 'Thanks, by the way.'

'For what?'

'Helping out.' He held the door open and stood, allowing her to go ahead of him.

'I'm sure you'd have coped.'

'I'm sure I would, but it would have taken longer, and both patients were distressed as it was. I'm grateful.'

'No problem. I had to start some time. I'm just glad I was around.' She gave a slight smile. 'At least I managed not to lose my first patient.'

His blue eyes glittered. 'I'm not going to be allowed to forget that, am I?'

'Probably not.'

They walked to the main doors, and she stopped to put her jacket on, seeing that it was raining heavily now. 'Oh, well, it looks as if summer is definitely over.'

Sam followed her across the car park. Hurrying towards her car, her foot slipped on a pile of wet leaves. Their bodies collided, momentarily knocking the breath out of her. She rocked backwards and instinctively Sam reached out, grasping her upper arms and drawing her towards him.

'Steady now. We don't want any more accidents, do we?'

Beth felt the breath catch in her throat as a feeling of physical awareness swept through her. She blinked, confused by the unfamiliar sensation, then pulled her hands out of his grasp.

'Thanks. I can manage,' she murmured. 'I'm fine.'

'Hands off—is that what you mean?' His mouth twisted. 'Tell me, Doctor, is it just me that you have an aversion to, or men in general?' His gaze narrowed. 'Or maybe you already have someone else in your life. Is that it?'

His glance flicked over her and she was suddenly aware of her femininity in a way that was utterly dis-

turbing. Working with him was going to be fraught
with danger—she could see it coming.

'I have nothing personally against you, Dr
Armstrong,' she said, striving to keep a steady tone.
'I'm here to do a job, and I'll do it to the best of my
ability. Personal likes and dislikes don't come into it.
As for my private life, that's strictly off limits, but I
can assure you that I won't let it interfere with my job.'

'I'm glad to hear it,' he said evenly. 'But it's early
days yet. Don't be fooled by today's events. That was
just a taster. I've yet to be convinced you'll stay the
course, once the going gets really tough.'

CHAPTER THREE

'BUT I don't *want* to go to school.'

'Oh, Sophie, of course you do. You've been looking forward to it.'

'Don't.'

Beth looked at her daughter's flushed, rebellious little face and felt her heart sink. Don't do this to me, Sophie, she thought, casting a frantic glance at the clock. The last thing she needed was to be late on her first day at The Gables. And to make matters worse, it had started to rain.

'But we've talked about this, don't you remember?' Beth knelt in front of her daughter, looking directly into the anxious little face. 'You'll make lots of new friends.'

'I don't want friends. I want to stay at home with you.'

Beth smiled as she smoothed back a stray wisp of hair from Sophie's forehead. 'It's a nice thought, poppet. But everyone has to go to school.'

'Why?'

'Because…because we have to go to school to learn to read and write, and…and do all sorts of exciting things.'

'Why?'

Beth drew a deep breath. The hands of the clock were inching forward and it was taking all her reserves of patience to cajole her daughter out of her sulks and coax her into smiles.

46

'Your new friend, Louise, who lives next door to Gran, will be starting school as well today. That will be nice, won't it?'

'She's got a swing in her garden.'

'Yes, that's right, and she said you can play on the swing later when Gran picks you both up from school this afternoon.' Beth kissed her daughter on the nose. 'So, what do you say?'

'Will you come to Gran's house?'

'Yes, of course I will. I'll be there to collect you at teatime, and you can tell me all about what you've been doing at school. I expect you'll be able to draw a nice picture for Gran. She'll like that, won't she?'

Things were bound to seem a bit strange for Sophie at first, but once she had made new friends she would surely adjust to their new life, Beth mused as twenty minutes later, having delivered Sophie into the safe hands of her new teacher, she finally turned the car onto the coast road and headed in the direction of The Gables.

She felt a stab of dismay as she glanced at the dashboard clock. Surgery would have started ten minutes ago. She could just imagine what Sam Armstrong would have to say about that.

She shook her head as though that might clear the image. This was the very last thing she had wanted to happen, especially on her very first day. It was almost as if the fates were deliberately conspiring against her.

'Sorry I'm late.' Breathlessly, Beth hurried into Reception and put her briefcase on the floor. Her cheeks were flushed and she had the beginnings of a tension headache. 'I had to persuade Sophie that she really did want to go to school.'

'Took some convincing, did she?'

'A lot.'

Maggie grinned. 'I know what it's like. I went through the same with my youngest. I found a little bribery works remarkably well.'

'I just didn't want to be late today of all days.'

'Don't worry about it. It happens from time to time, especially if one of the doctors has to do an urgent house call before surgery. The patients are a pretty understanding bunch.'

Beth couldn't help thinking that Sam wasn't likely to be quite so obliging.

'I'd better make a start. I take it Sam's well ahead of me?'

'Oh, he's nearly always in early. He reckons he can get through more paperwork in the half-hour before surgery starts than the whole of the rest of the day.' Maggie riffled through the papers on her desk. 'Here you go.' She handed Beth a bundle of case notes. 'All yours.'

'Nice!'

'Any problems, anything you're not sure of, just give me a call. If I can't help, I'm sure Debbie can.'

'Thanks. You're a star.'

The phone rang. Maggie reached out to silence it, cupping her hand over the receiver. 'I'll give you a few minutes to sort yourself out. If you buzz when you're ready I'll send the first patient in. When you've finished you'll find coffee in the staff room. I expect John will be in by then. You haven't met him yet, have you?'

'John Parker? No, I haven't. We seem to keep missing each other.'

'He's doing his visits now, but he'll be back later.'

'Great.' Beth smiled. 'I look forward to catching up with him.'

With a wave of her hand she set off down the corridor. Glancing briefly at the notes of her first patient, she didn't see Sam come out of his room until she almost collided with him.

'Oh, I'm sorry.'

His mouth made a grim line and she swallowed hard, readying herself for the blast. 'You decided to join us, then,' he said tersely. 'I was beginning to think you'd changed your mind.'

'I really am sorry,' she said, adding with quiet defensiveness, 'I thought I had everything under control, then Sophie decided to have a last-minute attack of nerves at the prospect of starting her new school. I could hardly just walk away.'

'I was given to understand that you'd sorted out your domestic arrangements.'

'I have,' she retorted, stiffly defensive. 'As it happens, my mother's nextdoor neighbour is a registered childminder. Her daughter is the same age as Sophie and they'll be in the same class at school, so she's agreed to look after Sophie for me when I'm working. Mum will have her when I'm on emergency call at night.'

She glared at him. 'I'm doing the best I can. I suppose everything in your own life is orderly and predictable and wouldn't dare to upset your tidy schedule, would it? Well, bully for you, but I'm afraid children can't be fitted neatly into pigeon-holes, however convenient it might be.' She broke off. 'I'm sorry,' she said curtly, looking down at her damp legs. 'This is hardly the impression I wanted to create on my first day? I must look like a wreck.'

Sam's hard glance flashed along the length of her shapely legs. She thought he was going to say something because his whole body was still for a moment and his lips parted slightly, but then he blinked and shook his head.

'You look fine to me.' He raked a hand through his hair. 'Look, I'm sorry if I seem short-tempered. It isn't your fault and I've no right to take things out on you. The fact is, I've just had a hospital report, the results of some tests on a patient who delayed seeking treatment.' He frowned. 'I think he thought if he ignored the symptoms long enough they might go away. Unfortunately they didn't, and now it's probably too late.'

'I'm sorry,' she murmured. 'I know how you must feel. It doesn't get any easier, does it? And I can see that me being late didn't help. I'll try to make sure it doesn't happen again.'

'You mentioned that you're renting a property.'

'Yes, that's right. A small cottage, overlooking the harbour. I was lucky to find it. Well, actually, my parents found it. I couldn't believe it when they told me. It's perfect. Just the right size for Sophie and me. The garden is small, but we can get down to the beach and Sophie's in her element.' Except when it comes to going to school, she thought.

'So there are just the two of you, then? No one else lives with you?'

She didn't answer for a moment, and he sent her an oblique glance. 'I'm sorry. I don't want to intrude on personal territory. I shouldn't have asked. It's just that you did say it was two years since your husband died. I know things can't have been easy for you but, no matter what you felt for him, time does have a habit of moving on.'

'I'm sure you're right but, in answer to your question, no, there isn't anyone else. I'm not looking for any kind of involvement. I'm happy with the way things are. I have my work and Sophie. That's all I need.'

She had no inclination to form any kind of attachment to a man. Experience had taught her that it was an experience fraught with trouble. It was something she could do without. Besides, it had been so long since she had enjoyed any kind of social life, she was sure it would be far too nerve-racking an experience.

'You can't have been married very long.'

'Just over four years. Sophie was just three when—' She broke off.

'I'm sorry. That's no time at all.' There was a note of compassion and understanding in his voice. 'Had he been ill?'

'No.' She marvelled at how calmly she was able to say it. 'Tim was always very healthy. Something of a keep-fit fanatic even.' She drew a deep breath. 'His death was very sudden—and totally unexpected, which made it even more of a shock. But I've come to terms with it.'

'Did he have any family—brothers and sisters?'

'No, he was an only child. His parents live out in Australia.' She looked at him. 'You're not married, are you?'

'No. There was a time when it seemed likely.' Sam smiled briefly. 'I was engaged, but it didn't come to anything. Things don't always work out, do they?'

He moved aside to let a young mother with a push-chair pass them in the corridor, and Beth thought twice about asking him any more. She wondered if his failed engagement had put him off the idea of marriage altogether. Maybe he preferred the freedom of a bachelor existence.

He glanced at his watch and gave a wry smile. 'I suppose I'd better get on before we have a mutiny on our hands. If you have any problems or queries, don't be afraid to ask.'

'I won't.'

Sam raised a hand in acknowledgement as he walked away.

She made her way to her own room where she took off her jacket and took several deep breaths as she prepared for her first patient.

A young woman, slim and slightly flushed, seated herself in the chair by the desk.

'I think I've got a problem with my waterworks,' she said shyly. 'I keep feeling as if I'm bursting to go to the toilet, but when I get there there's hardly any water to pass. It's a real nuisance and so embarrassing, especially at work when I keep having to leave the office.'

'I'm sure it is.' Beth smiled sympathetically. She glanced at the case notes displayed on her computer monitor and asked, 'Have you had this problem before?'

'Yes, I have, as a matter of fact. But it was about…eighteen months ago?'

'Right. Ah, yes, here it is, Mrs Carey…Brenda. You saw Dr Reynolds.'

'That's right.

'I expect you know what the next question is?'

'Did I bring a urine specimen?' She handed over a small bottle.

'Great. I'll test this now. How have you been feeling

generally?' she asked as she carried out the simple procedure.

'Not very well, to tell you the truth. I've been feeling a bit queasy.' Brenda Carey gave a short laugh. 'At first I thought it might be a bit of a tummy upset. I think I've had a bit of a temperature, too.'

'I'm not surprised.' Beth washed her hands at the small wash-basin before returning to her desk. 'There's a trace of blood in your urine. Have you been taking aspirin recently?'

'No. I usually take paracetamol if I need a painkiller.'

Beth nodded. 'Do you have any pain?'

'Mmm. Sort of across here.' The girl's hand wavered vaguely over her lower abdomen. 'And I get a sort of burning sensation when I spend a penny.'

'Any backache?'

'Yes, down here.' Brenda's hand moved to her lower back. She pulled a wry face. 'It's not easy, sitting at a desk all day.'

'No, I'm sure it isn't. Well, I'm afraid you've got cystitis, and the bad news is that you may get repeat attacks. In future, if you think you might be experiencing the same symptoms, you should start drinking plenty of water. It will help to flush the germs out of the bladder and dilute the urine, which should make it less painful to pass.'

'That would certainly be a relief.'

Beth grinned. 'Keep on drinking as much water as you can for a while and I'll prescribe you an antibiotic.'

Brenda breathed a sigh of relief. 'What about painkillers?'

'Paracetamol are fine. You might find that putting a hot water bottle against your back will help, too. Give it a try anyway. If, after a few days, things haven't improved, come and see me again.'

'Thanks, Doctor. I'm really grateful.'

Brenda left the room and Beth pressed the buzzer to summon her next patient.

He was a man in his late fifties of stocky build. He looked rather anxious.

'Good morning, Mr Daniels. How can I help you?'

'I've got this awful noise in my ears, Doctor. I think I'm going deaf. It's a damn nuisance and I'm worried sick because it's starting to affect my work, and I don't want to lose my job.'

'No, of course you don't.' Beth glanced quickly at her computer screen as he sat down. 'What sort of noise is it, Mr Daniels?'

'Well, sort of a…buzzing, ringing, whistling.' He gave a short laugh. 'I'm not really sure. I just know it's there all the time and it's getting on my nerves.'

'You haven't had this problem before?'

'No.' He shook his head.

'And when did you first become aware of it?'

'Oh, I suppose…a couple of weeks ago.'

'Right.' Beth reached for the auriscope and rose to her feet. 'I'd like to take a look in your ears, just to make sure you don't have a middle ear infection. Or sometimes a build-up of wax can cause the problem.'

She made a quick but thorough examination. 'Well, they seem clear.'

'So you think I may be going deaf? It's down to my age?'

'No, not necessarily.' Beth smiled. 'There can be any number of causes of tinnitus. About one in ten people suffer from it at some time in their lives, but it's more common in people over the age of forty. One of the main problems is that you may have difficulty sleeping, which means that you'll feel more tired next day, which again can cause problems at work.'

'Tell me about it.' Clive Daniels gave a rueful laugh. 'It's been making me damned bad tempered. I'm not the most popular person right now. It's just such a nuisance.'

'I'm sure it is.' Beth looked at her notes again. 'You haven't been taking any antibiotics lately? Tinnitus can sometimes be a side effect of certain medication.' She frowned. 'I see that you came to the surgery about… three weeks ago?'

'Yes, that's right. I'd twisted my back, doing some gardening.'

'And you saw Dr Parker.'

'That's right. He gave me some anti-inflammatory tablets.' He pulled a face. 'I took them for a few days. They made me feel queasy so I stopped taking them. I didn't like to bother him again. I thought I'd take some aspirin instead.'

'Ah. Well, that's more than likely to be the cause of your problem.'

'What? Just taking aspirin can cause this noise in my ears?'

'I'm afraid so, especially if you take them for a prolonged period of time. You're obviously one of the unlucky ones. I suggest you leave the aspirin off altogether. Is the back still bothering you?'

'Not so much now. The odd twinge.'

'Well, see how you feel in a few days time. if you're still having problems come and see me again and we'll do some tests, but I think you'll find the problem will have solved itself.'

'I hope you're right. It will be such a relief to be

able to hear properly again, not to mention getting a decent night's sleep.'

Beth was kept so busy for the rest of the morning that it was almost a shock to find that it was nearly lunchtime. Having seen the last of her patients out, she was gathering up her briefcase and jacket when the phone rang.

'Beth?' her mother said. 'I haven't caught you at an awkward moment, have I?'

'No, not at all. I've just seen my last patient as a matter of fact.'

'Oh, good. How was Sophie this morning? I've been thinking about her. She must have been excited, starting at her new school.'

'Not so that you'd notice.' Beth bit back a sigh. She'd been thinking about Sophie, too. 'She decided that perhaps she'd rather not go after all. We had a bit of a battle.'

'Oh, no! But I'm sure she'll be all right once she settles in.'

'That's more or less what I told her.'

They chatted for a while, then Beth, detecting a slightly strained note in her mother's voice, asked, 'Mum, are you all right?'

'Yes, dear. Why?'

'You just sound a bit fraught. You're not…? Is Dad all right?'

'Well… No, not really,' she admitted. 'I am a bit worried about him to tell you the truth. He had another of his turns this morning.'

Beth bit at her lower lip. 'When you say "turns", Mum, what exactly do you mean?'

'Oh, you know, dear. Sort of breathless, dizzy, that

sort of thing. I did ask him about it but he insists it's nothing.'

'Mum, you don't get symptoms like that for no reason.'

'That's what I told him. Then he just got cross and told me to stop fussing. You know what he's like.'

'Yes, I do. But the only way we'll find out if there *is* something wrong is if he has some tests.'

'He won't be happy about that.'

'I know, but he does need to see a specialist, Mum, to get this sorted out once and for all. Look, would you like me to talk to him?'

'Would you, dear?'

'Yes, of course I will.'

Her mother rang off and Beth made her way slowly out to the reception desk and handed over the bundle of case notes, her thoughts still preoccupied with her father. The sooner he could be persuaded to see a specialist, the better.

Maggie grinned. 'You survived, then? How did it go?'

'What? Oh, quite well, actually.' Beth smiled. 'Not nearly as nerve-racking as I thought it might be.'

'You must be ready for a coffee.'

'Absolutely gasping.'

'It's in the staff room. Help yourself. Biscuits too, providing someone hasn't beaten you to it, of course.'

Making her way through to the staff room, Beth saw that someone else was already ensconced there, sipping coffee and glancing through a medical journal. He looked up as she walked into the room.

'So, we meet at last.' The sandy-haired man set his cup down and rose to his feet to greet her. Brown eyes twinkled as he came towards her. He was about thirty years old, of medium height and good-looking. 'The cavalry has arrived.' One eyebrow rose as he extended his hand in welcome. 'And such a nice cavalry, too. Dr Jardine, I presume?'

Beth laughed as her hand was clasped in a firm, warm grip. 'And you must be Dr Parker.'

'John, for heaven's sake. We don't stand too much on formality here. The staff wouldn't stand for it!'

'In that case, the name is Beth.'

'And very nice too. How about some coffee?'

'I'd love a cup.'

He poured coffee from a Thermos jug and handed her a cup before refilling his own. 'Help yourself to milk, sugar and biscuits. 'How's it going?'

'Fine so far, but it's early days.'

'Oh, we're a pretty friendly bunch. If you have any queries or problems I'm sure one or other of us will be able to help. The thing is, don't be afraid to ask.'

'I'll be sure to do that.' Beth sipped at her coffee, relishing its strong, dark aroma. 'I'm sorry I didn't get to meet you when I first came to look at the practice. Of course, I only saw Doug on that occasion.'

'That's right. I was sorry to have missed you, but I seem to recall I had a day off, and I think Sam was away at a conference somewhere.' He gave a deep-throated chuckle. 'Probably just as well or, between us, we might have put you off.'

Beth laughed. 'I don't think that's likely. The thing is, now that I'm here I do want to take my fair share of the responsibilities.'

'I'm sure Sam will be only too delighted.'

'And what about clinics?'

'The usual—mums and toddlers, antenatal.'

'Well-woman?'

'That, too. Kelly, our nurse, does cervical smears, blood-pressure checks that sort of thing. Obviously if a patient has a problem she'll refer them to one of us.'

'Sounds as if I'll be kept pretty busy, then.' She glanced at a journal on the coffee-table. 'Oh, is that the latest edition? I missed out on mine, what with the move and everything. There's an article I particularly wanted to read.'

'Help yourself. I've finished with it.'

'Thanks. If you're sure you don't mind.'

They both reached for it at the same time, colliding softly.

'Oops!' John's hands went around her arms, steadying her. His eyes were warm and friendly as he looked at her. 'Can't have you ending up in Casualty on your first day here, can we?'

She laughed. 'It probably wouldn't make me too popular.' Especially with a certain person. She batted the thought hastily aside as, on cue, Sam walked into the room.

He dropped a file onto the table and looked at John. 'Should you still be here?' he said crisply. 'I thought you had a list of calls to make.' His glance skated over Beth, his expression cool, and she felt a faint rush of colour into her cheeks.

John released her. 'I'm just on my way,' he said amiably. 'I was finishing my coffee when Beth arrived. We hadn't met before so now seemed a good time to introduce ourselves.' About to move away, he looked at her and said as an afterthought, 'We'll have to get together for a proper chat—now that we're going to be working together. Perhaps we can meet up for a drink some time?'

Without turning her head, Beth could sense Sam's

eyes watching her. The set of his mouth suggested that he was angry, and she found herself wondering why, what she could possibly have done to justify it. Perhaps he didn't approve of relationships between members of the practice. Surely he couldn't think…?

The idea was so ludicrous she almost laughed aloud. On the other hand, a spark of rebellion asserted itself. Just because he was, in effect her boss, that didn't give him the right to organise her social life as well.

She flashed him a look, before bestowing her nicest smile on John.

'Yes, maybe. I'd like that.'

He grinned. 'Right, well, on that happy note, I'll be off. Feel free to call on me should you need my advice.'

The door closed behind him, leaving her alone with Sam.

'You certainly don't waste any time, do you?' he said drily. 'I suggest that if you must arrange your social calendar, you do it outside working hours in future. It's hardly going to instil confidence in the patients if they see you in a clinch, is it?'

'I'll be sure to do that,' she said thinly. 'And now, if you'll excuse me. I wouldn't want you to get the idea I wasn't pulling my weight.'

Dismissively she started to walk away, but his hand shot out, capturing her arms and pulling her back towards him.

Angry as she was at his unjustified attack, a burning sensation coursed through her, leaving her feeling oddly dazed and breathless. She felt the breath snag in her throat as for several seconds she was held within the warm circle of his arms, and she felt the full weight of his eyes studying her.

His skin smelt faintly of expensive aftershave, and she was totally unprepared for the effect his touch had on her as a sensation of instant fire seemed to race through her bloodstream.

She stared at him, bemused. The blue eyes returned her gaze steadily, and he said softly, 'Take my advice. Keep your mind on your work, otherwise who knows what situations you might find yourself in?' Then his mouth twisted into a mocking smile and he released her, moving briskly away.

Beth watched him go, her nervous system leaping and jerking in chaotic disorder. What had she let herself in for? She didn't know anything about Sam Armstrong, except that he seemed to have the ability to provoke a great many emotions in her, none of which was going to make for an easy working relationship.

CHAPTER FOUR

THE weather took a turn for the better again over the next few days, bringing crisp, bright mornings and a spreading carpet of falling leaves from the trees. On the work front, Beth went out of her way to make sure that, at least outwardly, her attitude towards Sam was purely professional.

It came as something of a shock to realise that even in the short time she had known him, the impact he'd made on her senses had been sharp and thoroughly disturbing.

Had she been able to avoid him completely, she would have done so. Unfortunately, in a busy practice it wasn't possible, meeting every day as they did. Instead, she made a conscious decision to put up a calm front. Which wasn't easy when she was constantly aware of him in the background.

If it became absolutely necessary to discuss anything with him, she purposely kept her tone formal and businesslike, determined not to allow herself to be provoked in any way. Sam Armstrong was very much an unknown quantity as far as she was concerned, and she preferred, if possible, to keep it that way.

Walking into Reception one morning, Beth put her briefcase on the floor and fanned her cheeks with a newspaper. 'Gosh, it's lovely out there. I love autumn, don't you? It smells different somehow.'

'Long may it last,' Debbie said wryly as she came through from the office. 'I dread the thought of winter.

All those dark evenings, the freezing weather. I can't get out into the garden.' She shuddered. 'It's like having a huge, dark cloud hanging over my head. I can't wait for spring to arrive.'

'SADS.'

'Yes, I know it's sad. Worse than that, I know it's pathetic but I can't seem to help it.'

Beth smiled and shook her head. 'No, I mean it's S-A-D-S. It stands for seasonal affective disorder syndrome. It's a recognised medical condition now and it can be treated. Haven't you spoken to someone about it?'

'No. I'd feel such a wimp. I mean, lots of people feel depressed in winter.'

'Yes, they do. But if it really affects your life and the way you're able to cope with things, then it can help to do something about it.' Beth reached across the desk for a list of calls. 'Why don't you come and have a proper chat one day—when we're not too busy?'

'Mmm. I may do just that.'

Beth scanned the list of visits she was due to make. 'Is this the lot?'

'So far anyway. of course, I can always drum up a few more if you're really desperate.'

'Morning.' John deposited his diary and mobile phone on the desk as he peered at the appointments diary. 'None for me? Right, that's me off, then. Feet up in the garden with a nice glass of beer.'

Maggie chuckled. 'You should be so lucky. Here.' She handed him a bundle of cards.

'Damn! Foiled again.' He grinned at Beth. 'How are you settling in?'

'Fine.' She smiled back. 'At least I'm beginning to understand the system.'

'System?' John raised an eyebrow to glance at Debbie. 'What's all this about a system? No one told me.'

'Oh, it's you, causing trouble again,' she chided good-humouredly. 'Speak for yourself, Dr Parker. The rest of us are doing just fine, which is more than can be said for some.' She glanced pointedly at the clock. 'I take it you'll be making a start fairly soon?'

'You're a slave-driver, Debbie Watson.'

'So I've been told. You won't be wanting coffee and biscuits later, then?'

John gave an exaggerated sigh as he headed for the door. 'It's threats now. The things a man has to put up with.'

Beth laughed. 'You're impossible.'

'I know. But lovely with it.' It was his parting shot before he disappeared into his consulting room.

The phone rang and Debbie went to answer it. Beth turned her attention to signing a couple of letters. 'I'd like these to go in the post this evening if you can manage it.' She handed them over to Maggie and frowned. 'I don't suppose the result of young Katy Kendall's blood test has come back yet, has it?'

'I'm pretty sure I saw it…' Maggie shuffled through the papers on the desk. 'Ah, yes, here we are.'

Beth scanned the report and drew a quick breath. 'Oh, damn!'

'Problem?'

She glanced up and blinked hard as she became aware of Sam standing beside her. He was carrying his jacket slung over his shoulder.

She nodded. 'The results of Katy Kendall's blood test.' She handed it to him. 'It's not the best news, I'm afraid.'

He read the report and looked at her. 'Leukaemia. That's tough.'

She swallowed hard. 'It's going to be hard on the family, even though I think they suspected the worst. I suppose the only consolation is that at least now they know what they're facing and, in a strange sort of way that can make things easier—for some people, anyway.' She looked at him. 'You must know the Kendalls?'

'Yes. They're a nice couple. I seem to remember there are two children.'

'That's right. Young Katy is six.'

'I imagine she'll be starting treatment straight away?'

Beth nodded. 'The sooner the better.'

'At least we can offer hope—which we couldn't have done a few years ago. These days, thank God, childhood leukaemia has about an eighty per cent chance of recovery.'

'That's the message I have to try to press home. They need to be positive.' She looked at her watch. 'Time I was off. I've a list of calls to make.' She gave him a remote smile and turned away.

'Actually, I'll be coming with you.'

'What?' She blinked hard, shocked by his arrogant assumption that she needed supervision.

'Unless you have any objection, that is?'

'Well, yes, as a matter of fact I do. I can manage perfectly well—'

'I'm sure you can. I'm not questioning your abilities, but it will give me a chance to show you some of the short cuts in the area that you may not know about. You'd be surprised how much time you can save, especially when there are tourists jamming all the roads.'

Sam's reasoning was sound, but it didn't stop her from feeling decidedly edgy at the thought of his coming along with her.

'Do you really think that's a good idea? The waiting room is already pretty full. Doug won't be in till later and John is going to be up to his eyes.'

'I'm sure he'll cope,' he said briskly. 'A lot of them are waiting to see the nurse. Kelly's agreed to do all the flu jabs.'

He had an argument for everything, Beth thought as reluctantly she made her way ahead of him across the car park. She wasn't at all happy at the prospect of having him by her side for the next few hours, and she was pretty sure he was well aware of it. He was too perceptive by far.

His gaze slanted over her, the blue eyes glinting in a way that was far too unsettling. She felt the colour surge into her cheeks, suddenly conscious of a crazy surge of emotions that ran through her like a tidal wave as she forced herself to look at him. She preferred not to think about what was happening to her blood pressure.

She threw him a malevolent look as she unlocked her car, hoping, even now, that he might change his mind.

'You're sure you actually want to take a chance on getting into the car with me?'

'Why?' A glimmer of amusement flickered in his eyes as he slid into the seat beside her and strapped himself in. 'Were you planning to have your wicked way with me?'

Beth choked. He gave a deep-throated chuckle. It was a surprisingly pleasant sound and, in spite of herself, she smiled.

'You're incorrigible.'

The smell of his aftershave drifted into her nostrils. Dressed in a dark suit, the material stretched tautly against the hard muscles of his thighs, Sam looked powerfully masculine.

He turned his head to look at her with wry amusement. 'You don't get rid of me quite so easily, Beth. I think we both know things can't go in the way they have been, especially over the past few days. We didn't exactly get off to a good start. I know…' He held up his hands defensively as she began to protest. 'I'm not trying to apportion blame. But somehow or other we have to sort things out or, at the very least, call a truce.'

'I don't know what you mean,' she muttered, wincing as she started the engine and grated the gears.

'I think you do. At least let's be honest. You may not like it but we have to work together, and we're not going to be able to do that if you're on the defensive every time I'm around. I only have to walk into the room and I can feel the barriers come up.'

Frowning, she manoeuvred the small car round a bend in the narrow road. 'I'm sorry. I wasn't aware that was what I was doing. It's just that I'm trying to do my job and it isn't easy, not when I'm constantly being made to feel as if I'm on trial. I'm perfectly capable of doing my job without supervision.'

'Is that really how you feel?' He looked genuinely surprised. 'If so, I'm sorry. I'm not the enemy, Beth,' he said quietly. 'If I do seem to have been watching you, it's only because I know it isn't always easy, settling into a new work situation, a new routine. I just wanted to be sure you were comfortable with things.' He frowned. 'I've had the feeling that something was worrying you. You seem…preoccupied, and I wondered if there's a problem, something you want to talk about? You're not on your own, you know. You're part of a team.'

'I know that, and I appreciate it.' She deliberately concentrated her attention on the road ahead. 'I'm enjoying the work. I feel as if I'm beginning to find my way around.'

Sam was studying her, his gaze sharply perceptive, so that she began to feel discomfited.

'At least I'm relieved to hear that the problem isn't work-related. So, what else is bothering you? You *can* talk about it, you know, Beth. They say a trouble shared is a trouble halved. We're here to help, if you'll let us.' He frowned. 'Is it your daughter? Sophie?'

'No.'

'You were concerned that she wasn't happy about going to school. She's bound to take time to adjust, Beth.'

'I know that. But actually she seems to have got over her initial nerves. Sophie doesn't say much, but I think she feels... She's aware of being slightly different from the other children.'

Sam frowned. 'In what way different?'

'The car accident left her with a slight limp. Oh, it's hardly noticeable, except when she's tired. She can't always run as fast as the other children, but I think, as she makes new friends, she's beginning to realise that it doesn't matter.'

'Children are amazingly resilient,' he said softly.

'I know.'

'So...what's really bothering you?'

Beth drew in a sharp breath. She was slightly shocked to realise that he was so astute where she was concerned. It made her realise how little she really knew about Sam Armstrong.

It was true that she had been preoccupied lately, but the last thing she had wanted had been to give him a chance to accuse her of allowing personal problems to interfere with her work.

Even now she resisted confiding in him. He hadn't exactly wanted her for the job in the first place. She certainly didn't want to give him any reason to think his fears about her reliability were in any way justified.

With an effort she managed to smile. 'I'm sorry. I've probably just been over-anxious—wanting to get things right, that's all. Where are we, by the way? My first call should be around here somewhere.'

'A couple of hundred metres ahead.'

She peered out of the window, glad that Sam had taken the silently offered cue.

Their conversation revolved around the work in hand as Beth's time was taken up with her house calls.

They were mostly routine cases. An elderly couple who couldn't get to the surgery, a youngster with croup and a patient recovering from eye surgery.

'Well, that all seemed to go pretty smoothly.' Sam eased himself into the passenger seat after the last call and they began to head back to the surgery.

Beth gave a wry smile. 'I was lucky. I don't fool myself they'll all be that straightforward.' She turned her head to glance at him. 'Thank you.'

'For what? I didn't do anything.'

'That's not quite true. You were there. The patients know you. It can't be very reassuring for them to be confronted by a stranger.'

It was a pleasant drive along the coast road and for a few seconds Beth shaded her eyes and glanced at the

small harbour, experiencing a sense of delight at the
scene. A return of the good weather had brought a few
last hardy tourists. That was one of the things she was
beginning to love about Cornwall. It had something to
offer at any time of the year.

Beyond the sea wall, the tide was out, leaving a few
small craft moored on the sandbed of the harbour below.

She felt herself begin to relax and was aware of Sam
resting his head back against his seat. He had just
closed his eyes when his mobile phone rang.

'Uh-oh! Let's hope that doesn't mean trouble. Yes,
Dr Armstrong. Maggie!' He frowned and turned his
head to look at Beth. 'Tom Watkins? Yes, I remember.
He had surgery on his knee… We're only a couple of
minutes away from there. No, you did the right thing.
I'll call in to see him.'

'Is something wrong?' Beth said.

'Could be. Tom Watkins called in to say his wife
has collapsed. They're both in their seventies.'

'Any details?'

'Not a lot, but Tom's a pretty sensible chap. He's
not the sort to ask for help unless it's needed.'

Beth slowed, then took the turning he indicated and
headed the car down the narrow road, pulling up
minutes later in front of a small stone-built cottage.

She got out of the car, following Sam as he rapped
on the door.

'Doctor.' Tom Watkins greeted their arrival with obviously relief. 'Thank you for getting here so quickly.
I didn't like to bother you…'

'It's no bother at all, Tom,' Sam reassured him
gently. 'I told you—any time. It's Edie, is it?'

'She's in here.' He walked with difficulty, supported

by a walking stick as he led them through to the small sitting room. 'I don't know what's the matter with her, Doctor. She got up this morning as usual. You know Edie, never one for lying in bed.'

'I do indeed, Tom.'

'She didn't seem too bad. A bit slower than usual, that's all, but, then, at our age there's no reason to rush, is there? She said her chest felt a bit tight, that was all.'

Sam glanced at Beth. 'Has she actually complained of any pain, Tom?'

'That's why I called.' Leaning heavily on his stick, Tom pushed the door open. 'In here. She's lying on the sofa. I've made her as comfortable as I could. The pain started about an hour ago. I think she felt it earlier but didn't say anything. I knew something was wrong, but she wouldn't let me call you.' His eyes misted with tears.

Sam quickly rested his hand on the man's shoulder.

'Don't worry, Tom. we're here now and we're going to do everything we can to help. Now, I hear you're not feeling too well, Edie. Tom says you've got a bit of a pain in your chest. Is that right?' Sam moved closer to the sofa where seventy-year-old Edie Watkins lay huddled beneath a blanket. She was pale and clearly in severe pain. Beads of sweat had gathered on her forehead, but she was still conscious.

She moved her head restlessly against the cushions. She tried to speak but it was clearly an effort for her to get her breath and Sam said quickly, 'Don't try to talk, Edie. Just relax and show me where the pain is.'

One frail hand went shakily to the centre of her chest and moved slowly in the direction of her left arm. 'Here... Heavy.'

'All right, Edie. You try to relax now.' Sam's fingers automatically felt for the pulse in her neck. He glanced at Beth and she produced her stethoscope, handing it to him, watching as he made a gentle but thorough examination. After a few minutes he straightened up.

'What is it, Doctor?'

Sam looked into Tom Watkins's watery eyes. 'I'm afraid Edie has had a heart attack, Tom. But it's a mild one. I know that may not be much of a consolation right now, but we're going to deal with it. The important thing is to get Edie to hospital.'

The old man reached out shakily to grasp at Beth's hand. She held onto it firmly and looked at him, seeing the fear in his eyes.

'They'll look after her, Tom. She'll have the best of care and they'll be able to make her more comfortable.'

'I want to go with her.'

'Yes, of course you do. I'm sure we can arrange for you to stay with Edie at the hospital.' She glanced at Sam and he nodded almost imperceptibly towards the door.

In the hallway he said, 'Will you call an ambulance? I'll try to make her a bit more comfortable.'

'You're not happy about her, are you?'

He lowered his voice as they moved away fractionally. 'Edie's not exactly robust at the best of times. Her age is against her.'

Beth looked at him and said quietly, 'How is Tom going to cope without her?'

'God knows. Look, I'm going to give her something to ease the pain. Do you think you can persuade Tom to sort out a few things Edie might need—toiletries, that sort of thing?'

'I'll get onto it as soon as I've made the call.' She

looked at him. 'I wonder if they have any relatives living close by.'

'I think there's a daughter but I'm not sure where.'

'I'll see if I can persuade Tom to let me give her a call. Right now I'd say they need all the support they can get.'

'Good idea. Beth…'

Turning, she almost collided with his solid, muscular frame. He stared down at her and before she knew what was happening his mouth came down to brush briefly against hers. She found herself holding her breath as a strange new sense of awareness brought the faint colour to her cheeks. 'Thanks for your help. I appreciate it.'

She watched him stride away before she turned and hurried out to the kitchen to make her call.

It was almost an hour later and the afternoon light was beginning to fade before the ambulance was finally on its way and they made their way back to the surgery.

'Would you like me to drive?'

Beth nodded, glad to relinquish the responsibility. Climbing into the passenger seat, she leaned her head back and closed her eyes briefly, feeling suddenly very weary.

Sam drove in silence for a while and she was glad. Her head seemed to be spinning. Lack of food, probably, she told herself. But it was more than that, she knew. It was a combination of things—sadness for the Watkinses, concern for her father and a sudden, disturbing awareness of her vulnerability where Sam was concerned.

In the fading light she watched as he drove. She had been touched by his patience. Not every doctor would have spent an hour of his valuable time explaining what was happening to Edie, the kind of treatment she would receive—reassuring an elderly man that his wife would get the best of care. In effect, persuading them both to place their lives in his hands.

Such strong, capable hands. Memories of their forcefulness as he had drawn her towards him and kissed her sent an involuntary flush of anticipation running through her and she tried to drag herself back to reality.

'You're doing it again.' Sam turned his head to glance in her direction.

'What?'

'Frowning.'

'Sorry.'

His mouth twisted. 'You don't need to apologise. I'm not the enemy, Beth. I just want to help—if you'll let me. You're not worried about the Watkinses are you? I'm sure she'll be all right once she gets to the hospital.'

'Yes, I know. I was thinking they must have been together a long time.'

'Fifty years. I seem to recall hearing something about a celebration a few months back.'

'It's an awfully long time, and Tom seems desperately concerned for her. I couldn't help wondering how people cope after losing a partner.'

'You're a doctor, Beth. You know the rules. You treat the patient and stay detached.'

'I know that.' She gave a vexed sigh. 'But it isn't always that easy, is it?'

'Isn't it?'

'Well, what if it happens to someone you know?'

'Has it?'

She stared at him blankly for a moment before turning her head to gaze out of the window.

'Has it, Beth?' he said again. 'Are we talking about someone you love? Your husband?'

She blinked, his words jerking her concentration back. 'No, I wasn't thinking about Tim.' The thought startled her for a moment, and she found herself musing with a slight sense of shock on the fact that she could so easily have dismissed her husband from her mind.

It seemed such a long time ago that he had died, and even longer since things had started to go wrong for them.

She took a deep breath and, aware that Sam was still waiting for an answer, said bleakly, 'No. As a matter of fact, I'm rather worried about my father.'

'I take it you have a particular reason for being worried?'

'I've been hoping not—that it's all in my imagination.'

'But you don't think so.'

She tugged at the fullness of her lower lip with even white teeth. 'I'm not sure. That's the trouble. He insists that he's fine, but I know something isn't right, and I know my mother is worried, too.'

'It isn't likely that you'd both be wrong.' Sam took his gaze momentarily from the road to look at her. 'What symptoms is he showing?'

'Well, that's the problem. Because he insists he's all right, it's difficult to pinpoint anything specifically. But I do know he's been having dizzy spells.'

'That could be due to any number of things.'

'Yes, I know that. But Dad's always been so active. He's a keen tennis player—or at least he *was*. I gather from Mum that he's given up—hasn't played at all this summer, in fact, and that isn't like him.'

'Has he given a reason?'

She shook her head. 'No, but Mum said the last time he did play he complained of feeling dizzy and breathless and went to lie down.'

'And this had happened before?'

'Yes, apparently.'

'Does he smoke?'

'No.' She flicked him a glance. 'And he's not particularly overweight. Nor is he unduly stressed.'

'I take it he's seen a doctor?'

'Not recently. I gather the GP he was registered with died a while ago, but I'm pretty sure the last time Mum persuaded him to go to the surgery he was treated for an ear infection.'

'It could be a logical diagnosis to make,' Sam said quietly. 'It would account for the dizziness, but you obviously think it might be something more serious.'

'I think the problem would have resolved itself by now, don't you?'

His mouth tightened fractionally. 'I can see where your reasoning is leading. It's possible his symptoms could be due to an underlying heart condition. I take it he hasn't had any tests?'

She gave a wry laugh. 'Getting him to admit there's a problem isn't going to be easy.'

'Well, look, supposing you can overcome that hurdle, would you like me to have a word with Jim Elliot? He's a heart specialist.'

Beth felt her heart miss a beat. 'But... Would you? I mean, can you?'

'I'd be happy to. Jim and I have known each other a long time, and he owes me a favour. I'll have a word with him, see if I can get him to take a look at your father.'

'Oh, I'd be really grateful.' Beth's attention was distracted momentarily as they drew up outside the surgery and Sam brought the car to a halt. She turned to look at him. 'I know it would put Mum's mind at rest if Mr Elliot would agree to take a look at Dad.'

'I'll get onto it as soon as possible. All you have to do now is persuade your father that it's for his own good. Hiding his head in the sand isn't going to make the problem go away.' Sam smiled and she felt an odd fluttering sensation begin somewhere in her stomach, as though all her bottled up tensions were suddenly being released.

She looked at him, seeing the generous, mobile curve of his mouth, the faint lines around his eyes, and she felt a strange compulsion to reach up and touch his face with her fingertips, to run her hands through the silky softness of his hair.

Instead she pushed the car door open, hesitated and said, 'Thank you. I really do appreciate it, though I can't promise you won't be wasting your time.'

'I'll take that risk.'

She managed to find time to grab a quick cup of coffee before starting early evening surgery. As her first patient entered, Beth glanced at her computer screen and smiled. 'Mr Johnson, please, take a seat. Tell me what I can do for you.'

Trevor Johnson smiled weakly as he sat in the chair. In his forties and, if anything, slightly underweight, he looked pale as he adjusted the set of his glasses on his nose.

'It's this headache, Doctor. One of my migraines again. Like an idiot I ran out of my usual tablets and forgot to replace them. Could I just have a repeat prescription?'

Beth scanned her notes. 'I see it's quite some time since you last had an attack. At that time you saw Dr...Reynolds?'

He nodded and winced. 'That's right. It must be about eighteen months ago. I was hoping I'd got over the damned things. I could really do without it—now, of all times.'

Beth looked at him and smiled. 'Why now in particular? Something special happening, is it?'

'No, not really. Well, maybe—sort of.' He pulled a face. 'There's a promotion in the offing at work. I know I haven't been with the firm all that long, but I reckon I could be in with a reasonable chance. I know I could do the job. I have the experience. Trouble is, my age is probably against me.'

She laughed. 'What are you? Forty?'

'Forty-two, actually.'

'That's hardly old.'

'It is when there are twenty-five-year-olds, fresh out of university, all clutching their degrees, snapping at your heels.' He gave a slight laugh. 'It's a cutthroat world out there, I can tell you. I suppose I was damned lucky to get the job in the first place. I'd been out of work for the best part of a year, and I didn't like it. The thought of going back to that...well, I expect you can guess. Trouble is, there's always someone waiting to step into your shoes if you don't come up to scratch.'

Beth nodded sympathetically. 'Yes, I can imagine. And that may be the clue. What sort of hours do you work?'

'Whatever is necessary. There's no such thing as nine to five any more. We've just had new computer software installed, which is fine but it's meant updating the whole system.'

'Mmm. I can only guess what that involves. But the fact is you can't work under that sort of pressure for long without suffering the consequences. Yes, I know.' She forestalled his protest. 'I know the job is important, but you have to ease up a bit.'

He sat back, removed his glasses and polished them with a hanky before replacing them. 'I'll tell the boss that, next time I see him. I'm sure he'll be delighted.'

Beth looked at him as she handed over the prescription. 'I'm sorry I can't do anything about the situation at work, but these tablets should help with the migraines. They're a fairly new drug. They're fast-acting, which is the main thing, and hopefully they should help to ease the queasy tummy as well. Just try to relax a little. I know it's not easy, but that's the only real answer, I'm afraid.'

It seemed no time at all before her last patient of the day was being ushered in.

From her records, she could see that the slim, dark-haired woman was in her mid-twenties and married. She looked anxious and tearful as she sat down.

Beth smiled. 'Mrs Barratt, what can I do for you?'

'It's…' The woman swallowed hard and fumbled in her pocket for a hanky. 'I'm sorry. I'm still a bit shocked. I can't seem to take it in.'

'It's all right. There's no rush. Take your time.'

'I…I found this lump in my breast, you see.'

Beth was hastily reading her computer notes. 'You saw Dr Armstrong.'

'Yes, that's right—and he referred me to the hospital.' She sniffed hard, blew her nose and looked at Beth. 'My appointment came through ever so quickly. He—he says I'm going to need an operation.'

'A mastectomy?'

'Yes, that's it.' Julie Barratt's blue eyes filled with tears. 'He said it was probably inherited from my mother. She died of breast cancer. It's not that I'm too scared of having the operation. I'd rather not, obviously, but I realise I don't have any choice. The thing is...' She broke off. 'The thing is, if it *is* inherited, doesn't that mean that if I have children they may inherit it, too?'

'I have to be honest,' Beth said. 'There *is* a risk. We do know that breast cancer does tend to run in families.' She frowned. 'That doesn't mean that you should anticipate the worst. Did the consultant speak to you about the various options open to you?'

'I'm sure he did, but to tell you the truth I didn't take much of it in. I was too shocked. He told me the results of my biopsy. I heard him say it was a cancerous growth—something about a mast-mastectomy.' She shook her head. 'I just sat there, staring at him, thinking it was all a mistake. He must be talking about someone else.' She gave a short laugh. 'I mean, that sort of thing doesn't happen to someone my age, does it? It happens to other people—older people.'

'Sadly I'm afraid that isn't the case,' Beth said quietly. 'So, he discussed with you the need for a mastectomy.'

'Yes.' Julie Barratt's voice faltered. 'He said that, in his opinion, I should opt for a total mastectomy—removal of both breasts—because there would always be a possibility that if they only do a partial, the cancer might return.'

She glanced up. 'I can live with that. I'm scared, of course, but I know he's right. What I can't take in is the possibility that I might pass this...this awful thing on to my daughter.' She mopped at the tears which ran down her face. 'I think I'd rather not have children than put them through what I'm going through right now.'

Beth reached out to hold the woman's hand. 'I do understand how you must feel.'

'Do you?' Julie Barratt gave a slight laugh. 'Do you really?'

Beth said gently, 'About ten years ago, my mother was diagnosed with breast cancer.'

'Oh, look, I'm sorry...'

'No, it's all right. The thing is, she had to make the same decision that you're making right now. Whether to have the partial mastectomy or whether to have both breasts removed.'

'It must have been a terrible choice for her to make.'

'Actually...' Beth smiled '...she says it was probably the easiest decision she ever had to make. She opted to have both breasts removed. It was a complete success, and she knows she won't have to face that awful fear again in the future.'

'I don't think I have her courage.' Julie bit at her lip. 'And what about you? How do you feel, knowing that the same thing could happen to you?'

'There are very positive steps I can take to make sure it doesn't happen to me. I regularly examine my breasts to make sure there aren't any lumps, and I go for regular breast screening. You see, it doesn't necessarily follow that because my mother had breast cancer I shall get it, too. Medical science is advancing all the time.'

The girl dashed away a tear. 'I'm glad I came to talk to you. I can't think straight right now. I know I'm not being rational and it isn't fair to Mike—my husband.'

'I'm sure he understands,' Beth sympathised. 'The

best thing is to get yourself sorted out. You don't have to make any other decisions right now.'

Julie rose to her feet. 'I'm grateful to you for listening. I just needed someone to talk to.'

'Come back and see me any time.'

The girl nodded and left, and Beth sat back in her chair, feeling suddenly drained. She hated this aspect of her job, this feeling of acute helplessness. Nothing in her training had taught her how to overcome the frustration and despair she felt on the occasions when she wasn't able to help a patient. She had always expected—hoped—it would get easier, but somehow it never did.

Beth closed her eyes briefly as she fought the wave of unhappy thoughts that threatened to swamp her. She thought about her father. He had always been so active. It came as a shock to see him these days, looking so pale and lethargic, and she knew he was becoming increasingly frustrated by the restrictions his health was placing upon him. Her mother, of course, made light of it, outwardly at least. But Beth knew that, deep down, she was seriously worried. Life was so unfair, disease so cruelly indiscriminate.

Without being aware of it, she sighed.

'Can you spare a minute? I did knock but you were obviously so deep in thought you couldn't have heard.'

Her gaze flickered up to see Sam standing in the doorway. She stared at him, illogically resenting the intrusion. She rose to her feet, trying hard to bring her feelings under control.

'I'm sorry. No, I didn't.'

'Maggie said your last patient had just left, and I wanted to catch you before you go.' He frowned. 'Is something wrong?'

'No, of course not. What should be wrong?' she said tautly. Without even being aware she was doing it, her fingers rearranged the items on the desk. 'Did you want something?'

'I did, but it can wait.' Sam studied her, a frown drawing his dark brows together. 'Beth, something obviously *is* wrong. Tell me,' he persisted.

'There's nothing to tell.' She moistened her lips, wishing there was some way she could avoid his shrewd gaze, but his hands caught at her arms as she tried to turn away. It was as if he had touched a nerve, sending tiny shock waves running through her.

The trouble with Sam Armstrong, she thought, was that he saw far too much for her own good. The last thing she needed right now was to add to his belief that she wasn't capable of coping. 'I really don't know what you mean. I just have a bit of a headache, that's all.'

'You're not a very good liar, Beth. Something must have happened.' His gaze narrowed. 'Has something…someone upset you?'

Not nearly as much as his nearness was upsetting her nervous system now, she thought. She stiffened, trying to pull away. It was crazy. She scarcely knew this man, yet he seemed to have the power to throw all her normally perfectly well-adjusted emotions into turmoil.

'It's nothing.' Her shoulders slumped. 'If you really want to know, I was just wondering whether we serve any useful purpose at all. I mean, for all the progress we make in medical science, something comes along and we don't know how to cope with it—we're completely helpless.'

'Oh, come on! You can't really believe that. Look,

ease up a bit,' he said. 'Do I take it this is something to do with the patient who just left?'

'Julie Barratt.' She swallowed hard. 'She's two years younger than me and she's been diagnosed with breast cancer. She was married nine months ago and now she's facing the prospect of having a total mastectomy. I doubt if you can even begin to imagine what she must be going through.'

'I may be a man, Beth, but I think I do have some idea. I'm not saying it isn't going to be traumatic, but presumably you did explain to her that the prognosis is excellent.'

'Oh, good!' Her eyes blazed. 'Well, that's all right, then. I'm sure that will make her feel a lot better.' She broke off, feeling the tears well up in her eyes, willing them not to fall. 'Aren't you being just a little simplistic?' she snapped restively.

'I hope not. I'm just not sure what you expect of yourself, or of me. Why are you blaming yourself? You didn't cause her condition. You didn't make the diagnosis.'

'It just seems so damned unfair.'

'Life is unfair. But I still say there's every chance she'll be able to lead a perfectly normal, healthy life.'

'Except that she may not have children.'

Sam frowned. 'There's no reason at all why she shouldn't have children. The mastectomy won't affect her ability to become pregnant.'

'I explained that to her—but Julie is afraid that she might pass on the tendency to her own daughter. They've just moved into a new house. They were planning on having a family, and now she feels as if her world is falling apart, and I sat there, mouthing platitudes. What sort of doctor does that make me?'

'You're not being rational, Beth.' She opened her mouth to protest, and he said firmly, 'Julie Barratt has to weight up the facts, based on the advice she's been given. The choice is hers to make—not yours.'

He looked at her, his features harsh, unsmiling. 'You'll have to toughen up if you want to survive in this job, Beth. We're doctors, we do the best we can. Sometimes it's not enough, but we can't perform miracles. You said yourself, our knowledge is increasing all the time. That's something to be positive about. Julie will get the best of medical care. There's every reason to suppose she'll make a full recovery.'

'You make it all sound so simple.'

'I didn't say that.'

'No. I'm sorry. I let it get to me. I suppose the fact that my mother was diagnosed with breast cancer some years ago somehow made this case a bit personal. I didn't mean to get over-emotional. I promise I'll try not to let it happen again.' A faint smile touched her lips before it was tinged with sadness.

Sam said quietly, 'I'm sorry.'

'Oh, it's all right. She's fine.'

'But now you're worried about your father. That's understandable, but it's a mistake to let your anxiety colour your attitude to your work. You're allowing yourself to become emotionally involved, and it's no wonder, with all the demands of a new job, and Sophie to care for. You should try to unwind a little.'

She smiled. 'I'm fine.'

'I don't think so. You have to learn to be a little easier on yourself—to relax—and I think I may have the answer. There's a nice, cosy little pub down by the harbour. The food's good, nothing too fancy, but—'

Beth stiffened. 'I don't need taking in hand. I'm perfectly capable of organising my life.'

'I'm not disputing that. I'm just saying it would do you good to think about something other than work. What do you say, Beth? Do we have a date?'

She thought about it for all of thirty seconds before answering. 'It's a nice idea,' she said slowly, 'and it's kind of you to think of it. But I don't think so. I'm out of practice. I haven't done much socialising for a while, and I don't think I'm ready for it yet. Besides, I think it would be better if we kept things between us on a purely professional footing. That way there's no danger of any misunderstandings.' She flicked him a look. 'I don't mean to offend you. I hope we can still be friends.'

His dark brows drew together. 'It's a big world out there, Beth,' he said tersely. 'You won't be able to hide away for ever. Sooner or later you're going to have to face it and start living again. *If* you have the courage, that is, but frankly I'm not at all sure you're up to it.'

CHAPTER FIVE

SAM'S words rankled over the following days. Beth tugged open the kitchen curtains one morning and stood, staring out into the small garden. What gave him the right to judge her? Yes, all right, so she was cautious. But what was wrong with that? What was it they said? Once bitten, twice shy? Well, it was true. If you'd been hurt badly once, you didn't go looking for trouble, did you?

Not that one drink with Sam in a crowded pub would have led to anything, of course. She had let her imagination run away with her, and that had been a bad mistake. The thought set her heart thudding just a shade too quickly for comfort.

Besides, she had to consider Sophie. Despite the fact that she was only five, she was a bright child. It was possible that she could still just remember her father, and memories—if not of the actual accident, then the subsequent pain and hospitalisation—might stay with her for a long time. She'd had a lot to contend with in her short life and as a result their relationship was extremely close.

Beth had, of necessity, become the main, strong anchor in her daughter's life. How would Sophie react if Beth began going out with men? She was already beginning to ask why she didn't have a daddy. Sooner or later, Beth knew, she was going to have to deal with the situation, explain about Tim and the accident in as neutral a way as possible.

'Mummy! Come on. Aren't you ready yet? Let's go.'

With a start, Beth turned to smile at her daughter who was struggling into a bright red mac.

She grinned, kneeling to help ease Sophie's arm into the sleeve. 'Yes, I'm ready. Did you find your wellies? And your scarf and gloves?'

'I don't need my gloves.'

'Yes, you do.' Beth kissed the tip of Sophie's nose. 'It'll be cold on the beach. Ah, here they are.' She delved into the pocket of the mac and produced the gloves. 'There you go. No, sit down and let me help you on with your wellies.'

'I can do it.'

'Right. I'll just go and find my jacket.' She smiled as she watched Sophie sit on the floor, tugging determinedly at the red boots.

Shrugging herself into her own jacket, Beth caught a glimpse of her reflection in the mirror. She was wearing boots and trousers and a heavy sweater, conscious that the temperature outside was dropping like a stone.

I must be mad, she thought, heading for the beach in this weather. But having lived in a large town, Sophie had been so excited by the discovery of the small cove. Being able to splash in the rock pools and walk on the pebbles. Seeing the water come closer and closer was her idea of heaven.

'Mummy, Teddy wants to go to the beach too.'

Beth gave a small sigh. Oh, well, why not?

She was hunting for her own gloves and keys when the doorbell rang. 'Damn. Now who on earth can that be?' She went to open it and felt her heart give a tiny, unaccustomed jerk. 'Sam!'

The faint smell of aftershave drifted into her nostrils.

He was casually dressed in denim jeans, the material stretched taut against the hard muscles of his thighs. He looked powerfully masculine.

'Hi.' He smiled wryly. 'I know it's your weekend off. I was hoping we might have a chat, but I see you're about to go out.'

Sophie moved closer, slipping one small hand into Beth's as she stared up at him. 'What's your name?'

'Sophie! You mustn't—'

'It's all right. My name's Sam. I work with your mummy.' He bent his knees and came to rest on his haunches in front of her. 'And you must be Sophie.' He reached out to stroke the teddy-bear's silky fur. 'He's rather nice, isn't he? What's his name?'

'George.' Sophie's lower lip jutted out.

Sam glanced up at Beth. 'George?'

'Don't ask,' she muttered.

'Ah! Right.'

'Mummy and me and Teddy are going out—to the beach. Come on, Mummy.'

'I'm sorry.' Sam looked at Beth and took a step back. 'I've obviously called at a bad time. Look, don't worry. I'll phone you later.'

He was no longer smiling, and Beth scanned his expression, noting the faint, almost imperceptible line that had etched its way between his dark brows.

'No, wait,' she said, 'You've heard something, haven't you? About my father's tests.'

He nodded. 'Jim Elliot rang me first thing this morning. He's had the results,' he told her, keeping his voice low so that Sophie wouldn't hear.

Beth felt her heart give a sudden jolt of fear. 'What...?' She swallowed hard. 'What has he found?'

Sam glanced at Sophie who was fumbling in her

pocket for a red rain hat, which she tugged over her curls. 'You were on your way out.'

'I promised Sophie a walk on the beach. I try to make the most of our time together.' She looked at him. 'Sam, I need to know.'

He nodded. 'Look, why don't I come with you? Or would that be a problem? I don't want to intrude.'

'You won't be, and at least we can talk.' She glanced doubtfully at his jacket. 'You do realise it's almost freezing out there?'

'I'll cope. Shall we go?'

'Are you coming with us?' Sophie wanted to know.

Sam smiled. 'I haven't been to the beach for a long time. Is it all right if I come with you? Mummy and I can look for some nice shells for you to bring home.'

'I 'spect it's all right.'

They walked down to the cove, with Sophie running excitedly ahead of them. The air was crisp and cold but invigorating, and Sam dug his hands into the pockets of his jacket.

Minutes later they stood on the shingle beach, watching Sophie as she began to explore the small rock pools with her fishing net. She glanced in Beth's direction.

'Mummy, you're supposed to be collecting shells,' she said accusingly. 'Lots and lots of shells. Nice big ones.'

Beth smiled and waved and bent to make a pretence of sifting through the mounds of shingle. Sam followed suit and she looked at him. 'Tell me what Jim Elliot said.' Her mouth was dry. 'There *is* a problem, isn't there? You wouldn't have come to see me otherwise.'

'Yes, there is a problem.'

Her stomach muscles clenched. 'Is it…is it his heart?'

'I'm afraid so.'

She drew a deep breath and straightened up unsteadily, shivering not only from the cold. 'I knew it had to be.' She wrapped her arms around her in a self-protective embrace. 'He never complains but Mum's known for some time that he's been getting steadily worse. The attacks of dizziness and tiredness have been happening too often, and she's sure he's been getting chest pain, even though he denies it.' She looked at him. 'Are we looking at the possibility that he may need to have a pacemaker fitted?'

'I'm afraid it's a bit more serious than that, Beth,' he said quietly. 'Jim was very thorough, as you might expect. He did blood tests, an ECG, an angiography and X-rays of the lungs. I'm afraid the results all point to heart-valve disease. Your father is going to need surgery. I've spoken to Jim and he'd like to operate as soon as possible. Do you think you'll be able to persuade your father to agree?'

'I'll have to.' She passed her tongue over her dry lips as she struggled to come to terms with the news she had almost expected but didn't want to hear. She swayed and was held instantly as Sam's hands reached out at once to grasp her arms, firm and gently supportive.

Just then Sophie came running towards them. 'Mummy, come and see what I found.' She held out the net. 'It's got legs.'

Sam released Beth and she shuddered. With an effort she managed to force a smile. 'I'm not sure I want to see.'

Sam took his cue. 'Shall I take a look?'

'Feel free.'

He peered inside the net. 'Wow! That's a crab. He's

a fine fellow, isn't he? Look at his legs.' Sam eased the small crab out of the net and held it in the palm of his hand.

Sophie watched as it struggled, decided she didn't like it and backed away. 'Put it back in the water.'

'Good idea.' Sam bent to release the crab into a pool. 'There you go.' He straightened up. 'There's a cave over there. Have you seen it?'

'What's a cave?'

'Well, it's like a tunnel under the rocks. Come on, I'll show you.'

'I didn't know there was a cave.' Beth trudged over the shingle beside him.

'It's fairly well hidden. Look, there.'

'Look, Mummy.' Sophie headed for the cave entrance. 'It's like a big house.'

Beth watched anxiously. 'Is it safe?'

'It doesn't go back too far, and the tide's out. Sophie will be fine, and at least it's sheltered here.' He turned to look at her. 'I'm sorry I had to break the bad news. I know how you must feel,' he said gently. 'But the prognosis is good. You need to remember that.'

'I was half expecting it,' she said huskily. 'I've been trying to tell myself it couldn't be anything serious, but deep down I was afraid it might be.'

'From the way you describe them, I'd say the symptoms are fairly classic for mitral stenosis. The shortness of breath, irregular heart rhythm, fatigue and weakness and so on.'

The wind whipped at Beth's hair and her hands shook as she pushed the errant strands from her eyes. She watched as Sophie ran towards the water's edge, bending to scoop up handfuls of shingle, letting them run through her fingers.

Sam said softly, 'What matters now is to get the operation done as soon as possible. Jim's a brilliant cardiovascular surgeon. Your father couldn't be in better hands. Try not to worry.'

'How can I *not* worry?' she forced out. 'Mum and Dad have given me so much support over the past couple of years. They were there for me when I needed them. Now Dad's ill and I feel...' Her fingers twisted restlessly. 'I feel so useless.'

'You've done everything you could, Beth. You persuaded him to see Jim Elliot.'

'I'm beginning to suspect that was the easy part.' Her voice shook a little. 'Platitudes come easily, don't they, when we're talking to patients? But this is my father. They went through enough trauma when Mum was diagnosed with cancer, and for this to happen now...'

'I do know what you're going through, Beth.' Sam's hands gripped her shoulders. 'I'm human, too.' His jaw was hard, controlled. 'In spite of what you may think, I do have feelings, too, you know.'

She drew a harsh breath, annoyed with herself for behaving like the over-emotional female he was so contemptuous of.

'Look, this is my problem. There's absolutely no reason why you should concern yourself. You've done more than enough already.'

She tried to move away, needing time to think. His nearness was confusing her. It would have been far too easy to walk into the warm, comforting circle of his arms, to let him hold her and soothe the hurt away. But he forestalled her. Instead, almost as if he had read her thoughts, he drew her towards him.

'Don't shut me out, Beth. You don't have a monopoly on feelings. Maybe it's time you realised that. Emotions aren't a sign of weakness.'

He sounded quietly angry. She moistened her dry lips with her tongue and looked up at him, her eyes widening as they focussed with renewed clarity on the tautly honed features, on the firmly moulded mouth that hovered just inches above her own.

She became conscious of the warm, masculine strength of him as he pulled her closer.

'Is it really so difficult to accept help?' His gaze narrowed. 'You have to come out from behind that barrier you've built up sooner or later, Beth. You can't shut out the world for ever.'

'I didn't realise that's what I was doing,' she said shakily. 'It's just that these past couple of years I've learned to look after myself and Sophie. I had to.'

She heard Sam's soft intake of breath as he drew her even closer, and she was shaken by the riot of sensations that coursed through her as with slow deliberation he bent his head towards her, his hand shifting slowly over her spine, drawing her gently into the heat of his body.

'It doesn't have to be like that, Beth. Don't be afraid.'

Easily said, but he didn't know the dangers. Looking up at him, she knew he was going to kiss her and it briefly occurred to her that she should at least make an effort to resist him.

She closed her eyes as his finger gently traced the curve of her cheek, and she felt her breath falter as the sensual mouth came ever closer, tantalising her with its warm desirability so that her own lips parted on a groan of frustration.

She felt his gaze sweep over the creamy translucence

of her skin and she began to tremble as his head lifted and for a moment he looked into her face.

This shouldn't be happening, she told herself. She made a soft sound of protest, trying to turn her head away, but he wouldn't allow it, pulling her closer still, if that was possible, until she couldn't help being aware of the taut maleness of his body.

'What are you so afraid of, Beth? You must know I'd never hurt you.'

Not intentionally maybe, she thought. The thought hovered. His mouth descended, brushing aside her denial as she clung to the rapidly fading remnants of her resistance.

The warmth of his body permeated her clothes, making her all too aware of his arousal, his vital strength. Then, to her everlasting shame, she stopped struggling as a totally new sensation surged through her, so breathtakingly exquisite that, almost against her will, she found herself responding.

She was lost to all reason as his mouth closed on hers and began to explore the softness of her lips with a tender possession that was unexpectedly sweet.

It was a long time since any man had aroused her to a sense of sexual awareness. Even with Tim it had never been like this.

The depths of her body's response shocked her and a tremor ran through her. She had never known such instant, mind-shattering awareness as this, and it brought a shadow of bewilderment to her eyes, made her stare up at Sam in uncertain dismay. She felt shocked and dismayed. How could she forget so easily?

'Please, no,' she breathed raggedly, her hand pressed against him as she tried to twist away.

Beth felt him tense. He stared at her, his eyes reflecting the battle that was going on inside her. Tension sparked in the blue depths, a glittering, febrile emotion flickering there, and she recognised it for what it was. Desire, she told herself. Nothing more, nothing less. The realisation was enough to bring all her defence mechanisms to the fore.

Sam had started off with the best of intentions, she was sure. He had wanted to offer comfort, reassurance. She had no one to blame but herself for what had happened next.

She felt confused and unsettled, dazed by her reaction to a man she scarcely knew, incapable of understanding fully the tumult of sensations she had experienced in Sam's arms. Pleasure, confusion—all the things which had led up to the kind of emotional battering she had promised herself she would never feel again.

She could hear the sound of her own heartbeat. It would be so easy to let go, to allow herself to be caught up in what was happening to her. But she had already been down that road, and it had led nowhere, except to pain and heartbreak.

She made a last, belated effort to draw away from him, willing the raw ache growing inside her to go away.

'Beth.'

She took an uncertain step back. 'It's getting late. We have to go. Sophie!' she called to her daughter who came running, her cheeks flushed, her eyes bright.

'Mummy, come and see the water.' She tugged at Beth's hand. 'I got my boots wet, but only a little bit.'

'We have to go now, Sophie. It's getting late.'

'Oh!'

'It's cold, sweetheart, and it'll be dark soon.'

'We can come again though, can't we? I like it on the beach.' Sophie glanced shyly up at Sam. 'You could come with us. He can, can't he, Mummy?'

Sam's jaw flicked spasmodically, his mouth making a grim line, and Beth swallowed, struggling to find her voice.

'Maybe. When it's warmer,' she managed. 'But I expect Dr Armstrong will be too busy.'

'I'm sure I can find the time,' Sam said quietly. 'I've enjoyed myself.'

'And we could find some more crabs,' Sophie said.

'That would be fun. Perhaps we could bring another net and look for some fish.' He bent to scoop up a handful of shells.

'Oh, yes. Yes.' Sophie clapped her hands excitedly, and Beth, watching the two heads almost touching, felt an odd jolt in the region of her heart.

Sam was turning out to be full of surprises. She was beginning to like him, perhaps a little too much for her own good, and it had been a mistake to let her feelings run away with her.

He was just a man, she reminded herself firmly. All right, he was an *attractive* man who, with typical male arrogance, had made a play for her. But that was all there was to it. She had been vulnerable and he'd had no hesitation in taking advantage of the fact.

She ought to have learned her lesson by now. She had spent the past two years trying to get her life back together. She didn't want to see it all ruined now.

'Sophie, we have to go home now,' she said, and even to her own ears the words sounded unnecessarily sharp.

Sam glanced at her, then straightened up, his height making her feel illogically even more vulnerable.

'I don't want to go,' Sophie complained rebelliously. But Sam brushed his hand gently over her hair.

'Better do as your mum says,' he remarked quietly. 'I think she's in a hurry to get away.'

Beth took her daughter's hand and began to trudge across the shingle, conscious the whole time of the brooding gaze that followed her as she made her escape.

CHAPTER SIX

IF THERE was one aspect of her job that definitely didn't get any easier, it was getting up out of a warm bed in the middle of the night. And why was it always on the coldest, darkest night? Beth wondered.

She could hear the frost crunching beneath her feet as she made her way carefully out to her car, her breath fanning white into the air as she fumbled for her keys and scraped the windscreen.

Not that she had been asleep. She juggled the keys and finally managed to unlock the car door to swing her briefcase onto the passenger seat before climbing in.

She'd had far too many thoughts spinning around in her head so that, despite being tired, she had been unable to relax.

Her father was going into hospital tomorrow—today, she corrected herself, stifling a yawn as she turned the key in the ignition and backed the car onto the road.

In spite of the fact that she knew that Jim Elliot was the best cardiac specialist for miles around, she still couldn't help worrying. That was the problem with being a doctor, she thought as she headed along the narrow country roads. A little knowledge was a dangerous thing. She was all too aware of what could go wrong.

The strange thing was that now that the moment had arrived her father seemed to be taking it all remarkably calmly. 'I know it's got to be done,' he'd said quietly. 'In a way, not knowing was worse. I knew something was wrong, and you know how it is, I started imagining the worst. These past few months haven't been easy on your mother. She worries. At least now her mind will be put at rest.'

Beth had hugged him and smiled, doing her best to hide her fears, knowing that she wouldn't relax until the operation was over and her father was safely back in his hospital bed.

She was worried, too, about having to leave Sophie with her mother the previous night. Liz Walker, her mother's nextdoor neighbour, had knocked on the door the previous evening and broken the news that she was going away.

'I'm really sorry,' she had said. 'I feel terribly guilty, leaving you in the lurch like this, but I won't be able to have Sophie after school for a while.'

'Nonsense.' Beth had fought to keep the note of dismay from her voice. 'It isn't your fault. You did warn me that you'd be going to stay with your sister for a while.'

'Yes, I know. But I hadn't expected it to be quite so soon. Her baby isn't due for another four weeks. It's just that her blood pressure is up a bit and she's been told to rest…'

'And obviously she'll do that more easily if you're there to help out.' Beth smiled. 'Of course you must go, and you're not to worry about Sophie. I'm sure I'll be able to make some alternative arrangement until you come back.'

Which was easier said than done! She hadn't wanted to bother her mother, especially now, when she had so much on her mind. But Anne had insisted. 'Of course I'll look after Sophie,' she said. 'I'll be glad of the company, and it will help to take my mind off things.

I love having her around the place, and Sophie likes being here. It'll be like a holiday for us.'

Beth had hated having to add to her mother's troubles, but in the end she'd had no choice. The last thing she wanted was to give Sam an excuse to complain that her domestic arrangements were interfering with her work yet again. He'd already made his views perfectly clear on that score, and she had no reason to think he had changed his mind. It certainly wasn't something she wanted to put to the test.

Without being aware of it, Beth sighed. For the past few days, whenever their paths had crossed, Sam had treated her with nothing more than cool formality and, perversely, she felt cheated. She had thought it was what she wanted, but suddenly she wasn't so sure. She felt bewildered by the conflicting emotions his nearness stirred in her. It was some consolation that at least they managed to work together without allowing their tensions to show.

Ten minutes later she pulled up at the Turners' house. Stifling another yawn, Beth cut the engine and climbed out. Cautiously making her way along the path in semi-darkness, the door opened just as she reached it. Sue Turner looked pale and anxious.

'Oh, Doctor, I'm so sorry to call you out at this hour, but I'm really worried about Jess. Come in, please. It must be near freezing out there.'

Beth stepped into the welcoming warmth of the hallway. 'You were right to call me, Mrs Turner. Where is Jess?'

'Upstairs.' Sue Turner was already leading the way. 'She's been a bit off colour the past couple of days. Nothing really specific. I thought she might be going down with a cold so I kept her home from school. But she woke in the night, crying and saying her head hurt, and then I noticed that she has a rash.'

Jess was lying in the bed, her eyes closed and her small face flushed. Beth put her briefcase down and sat beside her. Fretfully the six-year-old turned her head and whimpered softly.

Looking at her, Beth smiled. 'Hello, Jess. Mummy tells me you're not feeling well. Can you tell me where it hurts?'

A small hand wavered in the direction of her forehead. Resting a hand gently against the child's cheek, Beth could feel that she had a temperature.

Glancing over her shoulder, she said quietly, 'How long did you say she's been complaining of the headache?'

'She mentioned it in passing during the evening, but it didn't seem too bad. I gave her a dose of Calpol. It seemed to help, but then she woke in the night, crying. I came in to give her a drink and another dose of medicine. That's when I noticed the rash.'

Beth nodded and reached into her briefcase for an auriscope. 'I just want to take a look in your ears, Jess. I promise it won't hurt.'

Sue watched anxiously as Beth carried out a brief examination.

'Well, they seem clear. There's no sign of any infection. Let's just check your glands, poppet.' Gently she examined the child's neck. 'Yes, they're certainly up. Does your neck feel stiff or hurt when you move your head?'

The child nodded tearfully. Her mother looked at Beth. 'She did say her neck was hurting and she didn't seem to want to move her head much.' She bit at her lower lip. 'It's not...meningitis, is it? I wasn't sure whether I should have called the hospital, especially when I saw the rash.' Her voice held a note of panic. 'I knew I should have done something sooner.'

'Mrs Turner, I'm as sure as I can be that it's not meningitis.'

'Oh, thank God. But what about the rash?' She lowered her voice as they moved away from the bed. 'Jess is usually such a lively child. It's all I can do to get her to bed most nights. I've never seen her like this before and I'm really worried, Doctor.'

Beth smiled sympathetically. 'I can understand that, but if it's any consolation I'm always more concerned when a child is unusually quiet than if it's making a lot of noise. Did she have an MMR vaccine?'

'No, I was worried about the risk of side effects. There had been a lot about it in the press at the time.'

'Then I'm pretty sure Jess has a fairly nasty dose of German measles.'

'German measles!' Sue gave a short laugh of relief. 'But what about the rash? I was so sure it must be something more serious.'

'I can see why you might think that, but you did absolutely the right thing in calling me.' Beth smiled. 'There's one test worth trying if you're ever in doubt about whether a rash might be something more sinister. Do you have a glass tumbler?'

'A tumbler? Well, yes. I'll fetch one from the bathroom.' She handed the glass to Beth. 'But I don't understand…'

'Let me show you.' Beth touched the side of the tumbler to the rash on the child's arm, moving it gently. 'See? The rash fades. If it was meningitis, it wouldn't fade.'

'Oh! I'm so glad you told me. If only I'd known.'

'It's no problem.'

'So, can you do anything about the German measles?'

'I think you'll find the rash will fade in two or three days. You can carry on giving Jess the Calpol. That should help to ease the headache and neck stiffness. Other than that, I'm afraid there isn't much more I can do. It's a fairly common childhood ailment, and it's probably a good thing in a way that Jess has it now, rather then when she's an adult. If she hadn't I would certainly have recommended that she be immunised against it at about the age of twelve, otherwise it can cause complications in pregnancy later. So, just carry on with the Calpol, and I'm sure you'll soon see a definite improvement. Make sure she has plenty of fluids and don't worry if she doesn't feel much like eating anything for a few days.'

'I don't know how to thank you, Doctor.'

'There's no need. It's what I'm here for.'

Five minutes later Beth was on her way back to the cottage, telling herself there was still time to get some sleep before she needed to arrive at the surgery. The soft trilling of her mobile phone soon put paid to the idea as she turned the car and headed in the opposite direction.

Her patient, she discovered, was a seventy-year-old who had fallen in the bathroom, breaking his arm and giving himself a nasty cut on the head in the process.

By the time she had arranged for an ambulance to take him to the local hospital, then had spent some time reassuring his anxious wife that he would probably be home again the following day, it was some considerable time before Beth finally returned to her bed.

Exhausted, she pulled the duvet over her head and closed her eyes.

She woke to bright daylight, with a splitting headache and the horrifying realisation that she had overslept. Maybe because she'd had her mind on other things or simply because she'd been tired—whatever the reason, she had somehow forgotten to reset the alarm. Consequently, having phoned her mother and spoken briefly to Sophie, she arrived at the surgery having had no breakfast, as well as being ten minutes late.

Neither did it help matters when she paused at the desk to gather up her list of visits for the morning to find Sam already there, grimly contemplating his morning surgery list.

'Good morning,' she said, juggling her briefcase and a bundle of mail.

'Is it?' The laconic tone made her pause as she hunted for her hopefully temporarily mislaid mobile phone.

Frowning she closed the locks on her briefcase before she looked up at him. 'Well, at least I'm hoping it can't get any worse,' she murmured, wondering what had brought on his bad mood and deciding to ignore it. 'I hadn't planned to be late,' she said pithily. 'I was called out in the early hours of the morning and—'

'I know,' he said evenly. 'I heard you drive past my place around five o'clock. I recognised the sound of the car.'

She gave a slight laugh. 'I'm sorry, Doctor. I'll do my best not to disturb you in future.'

Beth felt an unexpected tremor run through her as he looked down at her with brooding eyes.

'It does seem to be becoming something of a habit,

doesn't it?' he remarked, a cool grimace twisting his mouth.

Beth glared intently at the attractive planes of his face, looking for some sign of amusement at her expense.

She drew herself up sharply. 'It was almost dawn before I fell into bed again. I think it was a mistake—falling asleep again. I feel worse than if I'd stayed awake.'

'So what was the emergency?'

'It wasn't, as it happens. It was young Jess Turner. She'd been complaining of a headache and then developed a rash. Her mother was afraid it might be meningitis.'

'And was it?'

'No, thankfully. She did the right thing in not taking any chances—I just wish it hadn't been at five o'clock in the morning, that's all.' She ran a hand wearily through her hair. 'I must have spent hours tossing and turning, worrying because I'd had to ask my mother to look after Sophie after school for the next few days, as well as having her to stay while I'm on emergency call. I know she's more than happy to have her, but I still feel guilty.'

'Yes, well, it goes with the territory, I'm afraid.'

'I realise that.' The note of impatient censure in his voice made her hackles rise. 'I'm not looking for sympathy. I just need my sleep, that's all, otherwise I can't function.'

'All of which, no doubt, explains your lack of concentration,' he remarked, a cool grimace twisting his mouth.

A look of puzzlement crossed her face, and he went on, 'I suppose it slipped your mind that you were supposed to see Mr Dunbar first thing this morning? He was on time. Early, as a matter of fact.'

Beth groaned. 'Oh, no. Mr Dunbar. I was going to do a blood test.'

'Exactly.'

'I'll see to it now. I'll apologise. I'll grovel.' She was already heading for the door.

'Kelly dealt with it. However, I'd suggest you don't make a habit of it,' he said coolly. 'I thought you had a childminder to look after Sophie?'

'I did. I do. She's had to go and stay with her sister for a few days. Her baby's due in a few weeks' time but she's having problems with her blood pressure so Liz felt she ought to go. Look, I'm sorry it caused a problem this morning, but I can assure you it won't happen again. As I said, I've made alternative arrangements for Sophie.'

Her mouth twisted in annoyance. 'Look, I don't know why I'm bothering to explain this. All right, I admit, I was a few minutes late, but I'll make up the time. It's hardly my fault if you're having a bad morning.'

She saw the muscle tighten in Sam's jaw and wondered again what had brought on his bad mood. It couldn't all be down to her late arrival, surely?

His own glance moved glitteringly over her, making a swift assessment of the soft blue sweater which clung to her feminine curves and dropping to sweep over the neatly tailored trousers which emphasised the slender curve of her waist and hips. She had dressed in a hurry, for warmth and practicality, but under that brooding glance she felt her colour beginning to rise.

Crisply, she said, 'Do you make a habit of taking

your moods out on everyone else? Or am I the sole beneficiary?'

He frowned. 'I hadn't realised that was what I was doing.'

'No? Well, maybe no one wants to risk getting their head bitten off for telling you.' Returning his stare, her gaze ran the length of him, taking in the clean lines of his expensively tailored suit. His dark, casually styled hair looked as if it had been recently trimmed.

She had to resist a compulsive yet totally illogical desire to run her fingers through it and disturb its neatness.

She swallowed hard. 'I have things to do before I start my visits. I'd better make a start.' She walked through to the small office to collect a pack of sterile gloves from the supply cupboard.

'Beth, wait.'

Sam followed her, pausing in the doorway. 'Look, I'm sorry. You're right. I'm not having a good day so far, but that's no excuse for taking it out on you.' His mouth made a wry curve. 'I'd scarcely walked through the door before a rep turned up, without an appointment, expecting to be seen before surgery.'

'And I'll bet he said he only wanted a brief chat.'

'How did you guess? He sat there for nearly half an hour. In the end I had to practically force him out of the door. I wasn't too happy, I can tell you.'

'I can imagine.' Beth almost found it in herself to feel sorry for the man. 'I take it you made your feelings clear?'

'Let's just say I think he got the message. He'll be making an appointment in future. Either that or he waits at the end of the queue. I'm certainly not about to start prescribing drugs I know nothing about, and

I'm not going to be won over by a hard-sell promotion at eight in the morning before I've had at least one cup of coffee.'

'So, I think we can safely take it that his day didn't exactly get off to a good start either?' Beth grinned. 'Look, I'm sorry, too. I don't know about you, but I could do with a cup of coffee before I head out into the cold. I'm not at my best until I've built up a decent caffeine level. What do you say?'

Sam glanced at his watch. 'Well... Oh, what the heck. Why not?'

They went through to the staff room where she poured two cups of coffee while he skimmed through the notes he was holding.

'Sugar? Milk?'

'Just milk, thanks,' he said absently.

She queried softly, 'Is there a problem?'

He dropped the cards onto the table as she proffered a cup. 'Not a problem exactly.'

'Can you talk about it?' She watched as he stirred the coffee, gazing into the dark, steaming liquid.

'I was called out to a patient who had collapsed at home.'

'Collapsed? In my experience that can cover a multitude of possibilities.'

'Mmm, I know what you mean. But in this instance she had literally collapsed. According to her husband, one minute his wife was standing at the kitchen sink. She complained of feeling as if something had hit her at the back of the head, then she collapsed. By the time I arrived on the scene and did an examination, her limbs were slightly spastic and her neck was totally rigid.'

Beth looked at him sharply. 'Are we talking subar-achnoid haemorrhage?'

'That was my diagnosis.'

Beth could see now why he had appeared so testy when she had walked into Reception. Clearly she wasn't the only one who found there were some aspects of this job that were distinctly unpleasant.

'What's the prognosis?'

Sam frowned. 'You and I both know it's not good. The first few hours are critical, of course. I rang the hospital this morning for the results of the lumbar puncture and they confirmed that it was a brain hae-morrhage.'

'Will they operate?'

'I don't know. That will be up to the neurosurgeon. The damnable thing is that she is only forty years old. She has a family.' He grimaced. 'There are times when I feel so bloody useless.'

'Hey, come on.' Beth gave a slight laugh. 'I thought I was the one on a guilt trip. It's hardly your fault, Sam. You said yourself, we're doctors. We can't per-form miracles,' she reminded him gently. 'You've done what you can.'

He sighed and put his cup on the table. 'Sometimes it doesn't seem enough, does it?' He walked towards the door. 'I'd better go and make a start, otherwise I'll still be here at lunchtime.' He stopped and turned to look at her. 'You said you had things on your mind. What things? Sophie? Your father?'

'Both, I suppose,' she admitted. 'I really thought I'd solved my childminder problem when Liz Walker, my mother's neighbour, offered to look after Sophie for me. She has two children of her own. Louise, her youn-gest, is the same age as Sophie, and they're in the same class at school, so it works out really well—or at least it did.' She gave a slight smile. 'I knew she was going to stay with her sister for a while once the baby was born. It just came as a bit of a shock when she had to go sooner than expected.'

'But you said your mother is happy to look after Sophie.'

'Yes, and I know she'll love having her. I'd just prefer not to have had to ask her, that's all, especially now. It doesn't seem fair. She'll have more than enough to worry about with dad going into hospital.'

'Maybe having Sophie to look after will be a blessing in disguise. At least it may help to take her mind off things.'

'Yes, I suppose you're right. All the same, it doesn't stop me feeling guilty,' Beth said musingly, then added with a sigh, 'There seem to have been so many changes in Sophie's life. I'd really hoped she would be more settled here.'

'Children are amazingly resilient, Beth,' Sam said. He pulled open the door and walked behind her to Reception.

In a moment or two a buzzer sounded and Maggie called for the first patient to go along to his room. Beth gave a sigh and turned towards the desk to smile at Maggie. 'I suppose it might be a good idea if I have a list of the visits I have to make.'

Maggie riffled through an assortment of papers. 'Here you go.'

Beth scanned the list and gave a groan. 'From the look of this, Sam isn't the only one who'll be busy till lunchtime.'

'At least he's in a better mood now.' Maggie lowered her voice. 'He was like a bear with a sore head first thing. No one could do anything right. I was always a bit scared of him when he first came here,' she confided. 'But that was before I really got to know him. I realise now that his bark is worse than his bite.' She grinned. 'Well, most of the time anyway. He doesn't suffer fools gladly, mind.'

Beth could believe it. She gave a noncommittal smile.

'I've always wondered why he hasn't married,' Maggie mused aloud. 'Mind you, it's probably just as well. His wife would need the patience of a saint. On the other hand, marriage might mellow him a little, don't you think?'

'I shouldn't think there's much danger of that happening in the near future.' Beth swiftly disabused her of the idea as she checked her pocket for her keys.

'No, you're probably right.' Maggie pulled a wry face. 'It seems a shame, though.' She lowered her voice conspiratorially again. 'I did hear that he'd been engaged once. I don't know what happened. I guess things just didn't work out. They don't always, do they? There hasn't been anyone since then as far as I know.' She grinned. 'Once bitten, twice shy, I shouldn't wonder. Or maybe he always ran too fast to get caught again.'

Beth managed a faint smile, but Maggie's words echoed her own thoughts almost exactly, at least as far as any permanent relationship was concerned.

With an effort she turned her mind back to work and said in a more businesslike tone, 'I have a couple of letters of referral here. Do you think you could get them typed up and in the post today for me? This one is particularly urgent. I want to get young Jamie Wilson in to see the ear, nose and throat specialist as soon as possible. His hearing is getting worse. He really needs to have grommets in his ears before he starts school, otherwise he'll soon start to fall behind with his lessons.'

'Sure, I'll see to it as soon as surgery is over. Oh, and these need signing. Then I can get them all off at the same time.'

'Fine.' Reaching for a pen, Beth scrawled her signature. 'Right, now I'm off before there are any more distractions. See you later.'

It was a busy morning but eventually Beth was able to head back to the surgery. She felt tired and cold.

The waiting room was empty and she made her way through to Reception where she dropped her briefcase onto the desk. 'Gosh, it's cold out there.'

Debbie glanced out of the window at the leaden sky. 'From the look of things, I'd say we're in for a bit of a storm.' She looked at Beth. 'You wanted these letters to go in this afternoon's post. Maggie just finished typing them.'

'Oh, great.' Beth scanned them briefly, signed them and handed them back. 'I don't suppose you know if Kelly's still around?'

'She's still in the treatment room, I think.' Debbie reached for the appointments diary and flipped the pages. 'Yes, her last patient left a few minutes ago.'

'Good. I'll pop in to see her before she goes for lunch.' The mere thought of food was enough to set her own stomach rumbling, but she tried to ignore it as she made her way along the corridor.

Tapping at one of the doors, she opened it and popped her head round. 'Hi! Can you spare a few minutes, or is this a bad time?'

'No, it's fine.' Kelly, the practice nurse, looked up and smiled. 'I was just tidying up. Here, let me move that jacket and you can sit down.'

'No, I'm fine, really. I just wondered whether Mr Jeffries came in to have his blood test done?'

'Jeffries.' Kelly frowned. 'Jeffries. No, the name doesn't ring a bell.' She flipped through the bundle of cards on her desk. 'No, it's definitely not here. Why, is there a problem?'

'I hope not.' Beth smiled. 'It's just that he was diagnosed with high blood pressure a few weeks ago. I've started him on regular medication, and he seems to be responding well to the treatment. As a precaution I suggested that we check his cholesterol levels and asked him to make an appointment to see you for another blood test.'

'Well, he definitely hasn't put in an appearance.' Kelly laughed. 'Perhaps he decided he doesn't like needles.'

'Hmm. Either that, or maybe he's afraid I'll put him on a diet. He admitted himself that he could do with losing a few pounds. A few *stones* would be more like it.' Beth shook her head. 'I think perhaps we'd better chase him up. I'm certainly not happy to leave things as they are.'

'Would you like me to contact him?'

'I think it might be a good idea. If it's just that he has a phobia about doctors or needles, he might feel less anxious if you have a chat with him.'

'I'll get onto it today.'

'You're an angel. Oh, Lord! is that the time? I'd better get a move on. I have to collect Sophie from my mother's later, and I've a mountain of paperwork to get through first.'

Beth went out of the treatment room and walked along the corridor. As she passed Sam's room the door was open. He was standing with his back to her, sorting through a pile of journals.

On impulse she paused and tapped at the door. 'Can you spare a few minutes? There's something I'd like to discuss with you before you leave.'

He frowned and looked at his watch. 'Is it important? I still have a couple of visits to do, and I need to call in at the nursing home to see a patient.' He didn't sound too pleased at the prospect of being delayed but, having taken the initiative, it was too late for Beth to have second thoughts now.

'It shouldn't take up too much of your time. It's about minor ops. We talked about it briefly but didn't get a chance to get down to the practicalities. I understand this practice has been carrying out minor ops for some time.'

'Yes, that's right.' Sam's dark brows drew together. 'There was clearly a need. Once we'd assured ourselves that we could invest the necessary time and money we decided to go for it. Why? What point are you trying to make?'

Beth took a quick, sharp breath at his impatient tone. She had obviously chosen the wrong moment to ask him anything. 'I've noticed over the past few weeks that Douglas doesn't do any minor ops, which means that you and John handle them all between you. It simply occurred to me that, well, that I could take a share of the workload.'

'Have you done any before?'

'Yes, I have.'

'So you know what's involved.'

'Yes, I think so.'

'In this practice we deal mainly with removal of cysts, moles, some suturing. That sort of thing.'

'I imagine it cuts down quite considerably on the time a patient may otherwise have to wait for a hospital appointment.'

'We've certainly found that the patients seem to prefer it.' Sam looked at her. 'Minor ops aren't everyone's cup of tea.'

Was he suggesting that she couldn't handle it? Her chin rose determinedly. 'No, I don't suppose it is, but I did quite a lot of it at my first practice and always rather enjoyed it. I quite liked the hands-on approach. Besides, I'd like to feel I was pulling my weight, and it would relieve some of the pressure on you and John.'

'Fine. Sounds like a good idea to me.' Beth barely had time to be astonished by his quick agreement before he went on, 'Why don't you take a look at the rota? We only tend to handle one or two minor surgeries a month. Emergency cases as and when, obviously. See where you'd like to fit in.'

'Oh. Right. Yes, I'll do that.'

Sam started towards the door and she followed him slowly. He stopped suddenly and threw her a sharp glance. 'Why so surprised?' he said. 'What did you expect me to say?'

Beth gave a faint smile. 'I wasn't sure. A little opposition maybe.'

'I'm all in favour of sharing the workload, Beth.'

'Yes, but...well, you have seemed fairly remote this past few days.'

His mouth made a wry response. 'I was trying to keep things on a professional basis. I thought that was what you wanted. Or did I misunderstand you?'

She stared at him and wished she hadn't as her eyes

encountered his mouth, firm and attractive and far too much of a threat to her peace of mind.

He said thoughtfully, 'I'm not at all sure that you know what you *do* want, Beth. I know you've had a tough time of it these past couple of years, but you have to move on, get on with your life.'

'I…I know. You're right. It just isn't that easy, that's all.'

'I'm not saying it is,' he cut in. 'I'm not saying you should forget. I know that isn't possible. But you have a life, too. I know you're worried about Sophie, but you're not responsible for the loss of her father. There's no reason why you should feel guilty because you're a working mother. Lots of women are.' He shook his head. 'You're doing your best for Sophie, and as she gets older she'll appreciate that. So isn't it about time you started thinking about what *you* need? Isn't that what your husband would have wanted?'

She swallowed hard on the sudden tightness in her throat. 'You don't understand.'

'No, I guess I don't. But I'm trying to.'

She stared at him, open-mouthed, shocked that he had been able to recognise her fears when she had scarcely even voiced them to herself, let alone to anyone else.

Sam's fingers moved to brush gently against her cheek. 'Close your mouth, Beth,' he said, his voice rough around the edges. 'Otherwise I may just have to kiss it again.'

She closed her mouth promptly, gulping in a swift breath. He said softly, 'You know what you need?' She looked at him and knew exactly what she needed. 'You need a change of scene.' He released her. 'I'm giving a bit of a party for Doug and Rosemary. All the staff from the practice are invited, and that includes you. It's all strictly informal. There'll be a number of Doug's old colleagues from the hospital.'

'No, I don't think—' Beth began, feeling the familiar sense of panic rising.

'Yes, you can, Beth,' Sam said quietly. 'And don't even think of using Sophie as an excuse. You said yourself that your mother is only too happy to look after her. Besides…' his gaze narrowed '…there's a reason why it's important that you should be there. Doug has decided to formally announce his retirement, and this seemed the perfect way to do it. So you'll be there, Beth, even if it means I have to come and fetch you myself.'

He started towards the door once more. 'I'm glad we managed to settle that little matter. Now I suppose I'd better go and do some work.'

'But I haven't said—' Beth broke off as he returned to grasp her shoulders and plant a kiss firmly on her protesting mouth.

'You're not going to keep arguing, are you, Beth? If so, I shall just have to keep on kissing you.' He released her again, a smile tilting his mouth, and she felt the rush of heat flood her cheeks. 'We'll make all the arrangements later.'

He moved away from her, and she stared after him, bemused by the strange sensation coursing through her limbs and leaving her feeling oddly helpless.

CHAPTER SEVEN

BETH tried not to think about Sam's party. She wasn't looking forward to it, but despite all her efforts to try to come up with an excuse for not going, she finally had to admit there was no way she was going to get out of it.

The truth was, she thought with a pang, that since Tim's death she hadn't felt the desire or need for any kind of social life, and the idea of meeting people, of having to be sociable, filled her with a sense of dread. The fact that everyone else seemed to be looking forward to it didn't make it any easier either.

Sam was right, she told herself grudgingly as he drove her to the hospital the following morning. She *had* forgotten how to relax. Two years of living on her nerves had had that effect, and it was a difficult habit to break, especially when, as now, she had good reason to worry.

Paul's operation had gone without a hitch. Even so, when Beth had seen him a few hours later, he had seemed so frail, so small and vulnerable, that she had almost broken down and wept.

Now, several days later, as she walked towards the ward and she could see him through the glass panel of the door, sitting in a chair and looking so much more like his old self, she still found herself thinking how close she might have come to losing him and her throat tightened.

Sam paused at the door and smiled. 'Give him my regards, won't you?'

She stared up at him, feeling an illogical sense of disappointment. 'Aren't you coming in?'

'No, I don't think so. I'm sure you've lots to talk about. Besides, they're pretty insistent on the number of visitors and we don't want to upset Sister, do we? I'll go and get a cup of coffee and see you in a while.' He squeezed her hand. 'Beth, I'm sure the worst is over. Jim Elliot is with your parents now, probably giving them a progress report and advising on a future health regime for your father.'

She nodded and gave a slight smile. 'I really am grateful, you know—for everything. You didn't have to drive me here today.'

'I wanted to.' His mouth curved into a smile. 'Let's just say I thought it might be safer. You're not exactly in the right frame of mind to concentrate on driving, are you?'

'No, probably not.' She gave a slight laugh. 'It's crazy, isn't it? I mean, I'm a doctor. I see patients every day. Some of them are desperately ill...'

'It's never the same when it's personal, though, is it? Look, why don't you go in and see him?' He gave her a gentle push towards the door. 'It looks as if Jim is just about through talking to your parents. They look happy enough. Go on. Better get it over with. Put your mind at rest.'

'I suppose you're right.' Taking a deep breath, she reached the door just as it opened and Jim Elliot came out, smiling as he greeted Sam before the two of them headed off together down the corridor.

'Hello, Dad.' Beth moved to stand behind him, her

arms round his shoulders as she kissed the top of his head. 'How are you feeling?'

'A bit bruised, tired. But, then, they tell me that's to be expected.' He patted her hand and smiled, and it was reassuring to see the twinkle back in his eyes.

She glanced at her mother who was sitting in a chair at the side of the bed. Her eyes looked slightly over-bright, as if she had been crying, but at least she was smiling.

'Mr Elliot has just been in to speak to us,' she said in a choked voice. 'He told us all about the operation.' Anne fumbled in her pocket for a hanky then blew her nose fiercely. 'I didn't understand all of it, but he says Dad is going to be all right. He'll have to be sensible, of course. Not try to do too much too soon.'

'Damn!' Paul gave a throaty chuckle. 'And there was I planning to run the marathon.'

'Dad, you're incorrigible.' Beth felt the warm tears of happiness sting at her eyes as she hugged him. 'I'm so glad. It's been such an awful, worrying time.'

'I take it you're all pleased with the news, then?' Sam said, appearing at her side. He smiled at Paul. 'I'm glad. I just spoke to Jim and I gather it all went extremely well.' He grinned at Beth. 'So you'll be able to relax now, and no more excuses about not coming to the party.'

'Party?' Paul looked questioningly at his daughter. 'You didn't mention anything about a party.'

She gritted her teeth and with an effort managed to smile. 'No, well, I have had a few other things on my mind lately.'

'You see what I mean?' Sam ignored the quick narrowed glance she shot in his direction. 'Always excuses. The fact is that Douglas has finally set a date for his retirement, and I'm giving a small party at my place by way of a farewell—even though he won't officially be leaving for another couple of months. We just thought it would be nice to thank him for all he's done for the practice, otherwise, knowing Douglas, he'll probably just sneak away. And it will give him a chance to make the announcement fairly informally. I thought, as Beth is now part of the practice, she should be included.'

'Sounds perfectly reasonable to me.' Paul laughed. 'About time she did a bit more socialising if you ask me.'

'Dad!'

'Well, it's true. You haven't had much fun this past couple of years. Time you let your hair down a bit.'

'There hasn't exactly been the opportunity.'

'All the more reason you should go to this party now,' her mother said. 'Your dad's right. You do need to get out more.'

'But Sophie—' Beth began.

'Will be perfectly happy with me. I'm only too glad to have her company, especially while your dad's in hospital.'

Put like that, how could she refuse? Beth thought crossly.

She was still brooding on it ten minutes later as they made their way back to the car park. Her mother had decided to stay behind for a while at the hospital, so that Beth found herself with no option but to climb into the car beside Sam.

Fumbling with the seat belt, a small pulse began to hammer in her throat as Sam leaned across to clip the belt smartly into place. She found herself gazing with fascination at the back of his dark head before he moved, and her gaze rose to meet the full impact of his startlingly blue eyes. It was a disconcerting experience.

'All safe?'

She took several deep breaths, thinking that she felt anything but safe. 'I'm fine. Can we just get back? I do have some work to do today.'

'Do I detect a hint of frostiness?' His eyes glinted. 'I'm sorry if I upset you.'

'Upset!' She almost choked on the word. 'You had no right. No right at all. I am perfectly capable of managing my own life, thank you very much.'

'But are you, Beth? Would you have agreed to come to the party if I hadn't pressured you?'

'I...I don't know. Maybe not...' She sighed involuntarily.

Instantly Sam's gaze narrowed. She heard his soft intake of breath as his hands came down on her shoulders, drawing her gently towards him, and she was shaken by the riot of emotions that coursed through her as with slow deliberation he planted a warm kiss on her soft mouth.

'Don't be afraid, Beth. You know I wouldn't do anything to hurt you.'

Easily said, but he didn't know the dangers. She closed her eyes as his finger gently traced the curve of her cheek, and she felt her breath falter as his mouth came ever closer, tantalising her so that her own lips parted.

She must have been crazy to think she could remain indifferent. The kiss seemed to plunder her senses. Desire coursed through her. She was appalled by her own weakness where Sam was concerned. But she had been

down this particular road before, and it didn't lead anywhere, except to pain.

She said hoarsely, 'No, Sam, I... Please don't.'

He moaned softly against her hair, releasing her
mouth for an instant only to claim it again. Her hands
reached up, her fingers twining in the silky softness of
his hair.

'I want you, Beth.' His voice was hoarse. 'You must
know that.'

She didn't want to fight the sense of urgency which
was threatening to engulf her. It had been so long since
her body had felt this kind of need, this kind of hunger.

With a sense of shock she realised that she was
within a hair's breadth of falling in love with this man!
If she wasn't careful it could happen. If she chose to
let it.

A sob caught in her throat and she stiffened in his
arms. She tried to drag herself away and felt his arms
tighten, saw the look of confusion in his eyes.

'Beth, what is it? What are you so afraid of?'

'I...I can't. Please, don't.' She closed her eyes,
aware of the turmoil in his eyes as she broke free, panicking as she realised how little it would take to make
her surrender. If he kissed her again... 'I'm sorry. I
won't be hurt again. I've been through it and I don't
intend to let it happen again, not a second time.'

Sam released her gently, his face taut as he looked
at her. 'You can't run away for ever, Beth. Some day
it may just happen, and you won't be able to fight it.
I don't know what happened but, whatever it was, you
have to start trusting someone, some time.'

She pressed a shaky hand to her mouth. 'I won't let
it.' The words were whispered as he drew away and
started the engine. He drove back to the surgery in

silence, but, Beth thought in sudden terror, it was already too late. She was already in love with Sam.

As the day of the party drew nearer she began to get more and more nervous, not least over what she would wear. Having surveyed the meagre contents of her wardrobe, the result was as depressing as she had expected. There was nothing even vaguely party-like which appealed—probably, she acknowledged, because of the associations they bore with Tim. There was nothing else for it—she was going to have to splash out on something new.

As luck would have it, she was off duty the following afternoon and, having popped into the hospital to drop some magazines in to her father, she made her way into town.

Having locked the car, she headed for the nearby shopping centre. Buying one dress shouldn't take too long, she told herself. Half an hour should be ample time. What she hadn't counted on were the brightly lit, festively decked shops, and it dawned on her with a sudden sense of shock that Christmas was only a few weeks away.

In the end, what should have been a quick shopping trip took a couple of hours and left her feeling footsore and with a decidedly reduced bank balance. But later, as she surveyed her purchases, she thought it had been worth it.

Saturday evening finally, inexorably arrived. Beth indulged in a leisurely soak in her favourite perfumed bath oil in an effort to make herself relax.

Twenty minutes later she stood in front of the mirror wearing the fragile lace undies which were also the result of her impulse buying. She was going to have to stop this, she told herself.

She had her makeup applied slightly more heavily than she would have done during the day, silver-grey eye shadow adding emphasis to her eyes, a touch of blusher for her cheeks and lipstick. Small hoop earrings caught the light as she turned her head.

The effect, when finally she stepped into the new red dress, was both dramatic and startling. A little too startling, maybe? Doubts came rushing in as she stared at her reflection, wondering what on earth had possessed her to buy it. She wasn't sure there ought to be quite so much bareness about the shoulders—but perhaps her thin gold chain might detract the eye.

Staring at her reflection, she realised that she must have lost weight, but it looked good, she had to admit. Even if it didn't, it was a little too late to do anything about it.

She slipped her feet into slender-heeled sandals, applied a quick spray of her favourite perfume and knew she could delay no longer.

Sam's house was about half a mile away. It was larger than she had imagined and lights blazed from most of the windows.

Pulling into the drive, she could see several other cars already parked and, stepping out to lock her door, she caught the faint sound of music drifting towards the garden.

Her heart was thudding as she walked towards the front door. There was still time to turn back. No one would notice. But even as she approached, the door opened and Sam stood there.

He ushered her into the hall and helped her to slip out of her coat, his fingers briefly making contact with her flesh. She couldn't prevent her tiny indrawn breath. An involuntary shiver ran through her as he studied her with penetrating intensity. She felt the glittering sweep of his gaze flame over her bare shoulders to the curve of her breasts.

'I wasn't sure you'd come.'

Beth passed her tongue over her dry lips, intensely aware of the musky tang of his aftershave. 'Did I have any choice?'

He gave a low rumble of laughter. 'Probably not.' Then, more seriously, he added, 'You could have brought Sophie with you, stayed the night. There's plenty of room.'

'I… That's very kind of you, but she's happy with my mother.' If she had thought him attractive before he was more so now in the dark tailored suit.

'Come on in. I'll introduce you to everyone.'

She could hear the steady beat of the music, the sound of voices and laugher, and she hesitated.

'I thought you said it was only going to be a small party, a few friends.'

'It is. Come and meet them. Remember, you're here to have a good time. Relax. I want you to enjoy yourself.' His gaze moved slowly over her, and she almost held her breath, wondering whether she should have worn something else, until he told her huskily, 'You look beautiful, Beth.'

Her skin warmed under Sam's heated, lingering gaze, and she said in a flustered voice, 'Thank you. I wasn't sure what to wear.' She glanced round her. 'You have a beautiful home.'

'I'm glad you like it. I'll show you round some time but for now I think we'd better show our faces, don't you?' His gaze narrowed as he held the door open.

'Remember, there's no need to be nervous—it's just a party for Douglas and Rosemary.' He smiled and the effect was devastating. 'That's not to say you won't get waylaid by the odd guest who wants to discuss his or her medical history.'

'I'd say that's par for the course.' She avoided his gaze. He was still too close. She could feel the warm strength of his body as he ushered her towards the lounge, one hand against her back as he held the door open. Sam was the most disturbingly sexually arousing man she had ever met, and his nearness was affecting her in a way she hadn't dreamed possible.

There were certainly more people than she had expected as they edged their way into the crowded lounge. The lights had been dimmed and music was drifting from a pair of speakers on the far side of the room. Couples were dancing, swaying in time to the music. Others were helping themselves from the laden buffet table.

Beth stood in the doorway, conscious of a sudden tension in her limbs, a feeling of blind panic that made her want to draw back.

Just when she had thought she was beginning to get her feelings about Tim into some sort of perspective, the memories came flooding back to haunt her. There would be no more embarrassing scenes, no more humiliating questions. But, irrationally, for those few seconds the thought of walking into that room, of meeting those people, was too much.

Without even being aware of it, she had half turned, her eyes widening, only to feel the gentle but firm pressure of Sam's hand beneath her elbow.

'Are you all right?' The blue eyes looked down into hers.

She swallowed hard, the momentary feeling of panic vanishing, to be replaced by a far more tangible awareness of the man standing beside her. It was ridiculous to feel safe with someone who, in every other sense, seemed to represent a threat, even though she couldn't have said precisely what that threat was. But the feel of his hand against her back was like a protective barrier, drawing her to him, shutting everyone else out.

Sam's brow furrowed briefly. 'I think I'd better lead the way.'

She followed, taking several deep breaths. Almost immediately he was waylaid, and involuntarily she found herself searching for his dark head in the crowd.

'Beth!' A glass of wine was thrust into her hand. 'We were hoping you'd make it.' It was Debbie, looking surprisingly different in party wear. Her face was flushed. 'This is Bill, by the way. My husband.'

Beth found herself shaking hands with a tall, sandy-haired man.

'Hello. It's nice to meet you.' She smiled, raising her voice slightly in order to make herself heard above the music.

'Same here. How are you settling in?'

'Fine. Well, just about. It seems to take for ever.' She broke off as John came towards them.

'I wondered where you were hiding. Come on, you don't get out of it that easily, my girl. Time to socialise.' Grinning, he whisked the glass out of her hand and swept her, laughing, into his arms. 'I thought I'd claim my dance before everyone makes a beeline for you.' He executed a complicated series of steps.

'I don't really know if I'm up to this,' she protested, gasping as he swung her round.

'Don't worry about it. I'll teach you. Just follow me and we'll have them standing in the aisles.'

'Roaring with laughter I shouldn't wonder.'

His attractive face assumed a pained expression. 'I'll have you know I was the scourge of our local disco every Saturday night.'

'I'm impressed.'

'I should think so, too. I've won prizes, let me tell you.'

'So has my Aunt Susan,' she gasped. 'And she can't dance either.'

There was something nice and safe about dancing with John, she decided, settling into the comfortable circle of his arms as they drifted round the floor. Nothing too demanding, either physically or emotionally.

The music changed to something more upbeat and, as if by mutual consent, they both moved from the floor, weaving their way towards the buffet table.

Unconsciously she found herself searching for Sam again. She saw him, deeply engrossed in conversation with a small group of friends.

She found herself watching, fascinated, as he smiled down at the woman beside him. About thirty years old, diminutive, blonde-haired, she had the kind of honeyed skin that any woman would envy, and the sight of Sam's hand, proprietorially against her waist, filled Beth with an emotion she absolutely refused to acknowledge as jealousy.

With an effort she wrenched her gaze away, forcing her attention to the person speaking to her.

'Beth, my dear, I've been trying to get a chance to speak to you.' It was Douglas, guarding his glass as he sidestepped a dancing couple. 'I'm so glad you could make it. Sam's really done us proud, hasn't he?'

'He certainly has.' She smiled. 'I'm sorry you've decided to retire.'

'Don't be. Oh, I'm not saying I won't miss everyone, because I will, but Rosemary's right—we deserve some time to ourselves while we're still young.' He grinned. 'Well, relatively young and fit enough to enjoy it.'

'So, what will you do?'

'We're going to spend some time with our family in Australia. We may even buy a place over there—if not, perhaps Spain. Somewhere we can enjoy some sun instead of all this damned rain.'

Beth gave an exaggerated sigh. 'I don't suppose you'd like a lodger, would you?'

He gave a low rumble of laughter. 'You'd be surprised how many volunteers we've had. Seriously though, my dear, I owe it to you.'

'To me?'

'You've fitted in so well. The patients like you, so I know I can leave with a clear conscience, knowing everything will be in good hands.' He glanced towards his wife. 'I'd better go and help Rosemary with the food. I'll see you later, my dear. Ah, here's Maggie.'

'Hi! I've been looking for you. I was beginning to think you'd given it a miss.'

Fat chance of that, Beth thought as she smiled at the girl. 'John's been giving me a dancing lesson.'

'Ah. Well, at least you're still on your feet. It's a great party, isn't it? Have you had any food yet?'

'Not yet. I was just about to,' She gazed in admiration at buffet. 'It looks wonderful. Almost too good to eat.'

'We'll do our best, though, won't we?' Maggie

laughed as they joined the crush at the table, Beth helping herself to food she didn't really want.

As the evening progressed, with the speeches over, everyone relaxed and several couples were dancing slowly, swaying together in time to the music. Amongst them were Sam and the blonde, her head resting against his chest, her eyes closed, his cheek against her hair.

'Well, well,' Maggie said softly. 'Look who's here.'

'Who?' Beth forced her attention to the girl beside her.

Maggie nodded in the couple's direction. 'I didn't know she was going to be here. But, of course, you wouldn't know. That's Tess. Tess Sinclair. I told you about her. She and Sam were engaged once, then she moved away. That was a couple of years ago, I think.'

'It looks as though they're still close,' Beth remarked with an effort, managing to keep her tone light, and wondering why her breath should suddenly snag in her throat.

The girl lifted a hand to run her fingers gently through the hair at Sam's nape, and he laughed softly at something she whispered in his ear. Watching, Beth felt a fierce stab of jealousy moving down her spine.

'You could be right,' Maggie agreed. 'I don't know what happened—why they broke up. They seemed such a perfect couple. Still, you never know, do you?'

'Is she a doctor, too?'

'Oh, no. I heard she was a teacher—somewhere in London, I think. Sam must have missed her. I mean, he seemed quite besotted with her and everyone assumed they'd get married.' Maggie frowned. 'Only they didn't. Suddenly the engagement was off and a while later I heard she'd gone abroad. Uh-oh. Here comes trouble.'

Beth did her best to drag her attention away from the couple and tried to concentrate on what Maggie was saying. After all, why should the sight of Sam's hand against Tess Sinclair's bare shoulder as he led her gently through the crowd bother her? She wouldn't pay them any attention—she would ignore them.

'Come on, then.' John arrived beside them, looking hot and slightly dishevelled. 'We can't have this. The pair of you standing around like a couple of wallflowers. How about another dance, then?'

'Not for me, thanks all the same.' Maggie warded him off. 'I don't think I'm up to it. Ah, there's Rosemary. I must go and have a word.'

'Chicken!' Beth called after her.

'Yes, well, you know what they say about discretion being the better part of whatsit.' With a wave she was gone.

'Which leaves you and me.' John held out his arms and, laughing, she went into them. 'Having a good time?' He nuzzled his nose against her hair as they made a slow, comfortable progress round the floor.

'Mmm.' To her surprise, Beth found that it was actually true. John had joked about his prowess as a dancer, but she found she was able to fit her steps to his so that they moved with an easy familiarity. As the beat came to a conclusion he swung her round, his hand resting lightly round her waist, and she looked up at him and smiled.

'Phew! I haven't danced like that for ages,' she said breathlessly. For the first time in a long time she felt exhilarated, free of tensions.

'Come on. I don't know about you but I could do with a drink after all that exercise.'

'Not for me, thanks. I'm driving.'

He studied her, his glance flicking over the delicate flush in her cheeks, the sparkle in her eyes. 'You should do this more often—smile, I mean. You look… different. It suits you.'

'I'm not sure I'd have the stamina. I keep reminding myself that I have to do a day's work tomorrow.'

'You need more practice, that's all. Perhaps we could do this again some time? Or we could go for a meal. When we're both off duty—'

'I think you've monopolised Beth for long enough, don't you?'

She blinked, then experienced a sense of shock as she realised that her early warning system, that nervous tingle that ran down her spine, had betrayed her as her vision cleared and she realised that Sam was standing beside her.

For several seconds, as their gazes met and held, she was disturbingly aware of him, and her already overworked pulse rate accelerated dangerously.

'I think we should dance.' His mouth made a firm, uncompromising line. He wasn't giving her any choice.

Reluctantly, John relinquished her hand to Sam. Beth's breathing felt constricted as they moved into the crowd. Why did this man have such an effect on her? And why did someone have to choose that precise moment to put on a slow piece of music so that, rather than dancing apart, he was drawing her closer, moulding her body to the lean, taut length of him?

She could feel the heat of his body, the thin fabric of her dress no barrier at all.

'Was that really necessary?' she muttered sharply.

'I think so.'

'You're cross with me,' she said. She could feel the tension rippling through him and found herself waiting for his anger to explode. 'Why? What have I done?'

His jaw clenched fractionally. 'I thought the idea of coming here tonight was so that you could relax, mingle, get to know people.'

She stiffened defensively. 'I thought that's what I *was* doing until you saw fit to interfere. Besides, I didn't notice you doing too much…mingling.' She couldn't resist the jibe. 'What's the matter? Did your friend have to leave early?'

He frowned. 'Friend?'

'Tina? Is that her name? No, Tess, that's it. Tess. The woman you were dancing with.' She looked at him. 'Maggie said the two of you had been engaged.'

One dark brow rose quizzically. 'Maggie gossips far too much. Tess used to live a mile or so from here. She's known Doug and Rosemary most of her life, so when I heard she was in the area, visiting friends, I decided to invite her along to the party. It seemed like the perfect opportunity for them to meet up again—and a nice surprise for Doug and Rosemary into the bargain.'

'Yes, I'm sure it must have been. Nice for you, too. I don't suppose you've seen each other for a while. You're obviously still very close. I mean—'

'Tess and I have been friends for a long time so, no, there aren't any hard feelings if that's what you're trying to say.' He shifted restlessly, his hand firming on her spine. 'Are we going to spend the evening discussing my personal life, or is there any chance we might relax and enjoy the dance?'

Clearly he preferred not to talk about his ex-fiancée.

Well, she was happy to go along with that. Now, relaxing was another matter altogether when his arms were holding her and his jacket brushed softly against her cheek.

He turned his head to look at her, bringing his sensual mouth dangerously close to her own.

'You're as tense as a wound spring. Relax. At least try to look as if you're enjoying yourself.'

Confusion brought the colour to her cheeks. She was trying to relax but his proximity was doing crazy things to her nervous system. She drew a long shaky breath, telling herself it had to be a coincidence that the moment he had asked her to dance the music was soft and romantic. He couldn't have arranged it that way—could he?

No. That was just wishful thinking on her part. Tess had gone. He was at a loose end. Don't read any more into it, she told herself firmly. But the thought disturbed her more than she cared to admit.

Maybe there was something to be said for making a strategic withdrawal. Beth stirred restlessly in Sam's arms and made a show of glancing at her watch. 'It's getting late. I should be going.'

'Why? Sophie's all right, isn't she?'

'Yes, but I'm on duty in the morning.'

He said softly, 'You could always stay the night here, you know.'

Her breathing was ragged as he drew her away from the slowly moving dancers into the semi-darkness of the hall. She glanced nervously at him. 'I'm not sure that would be a good idea,' she said huskily.

'Why, Beth? What are you so afraid of?'

'I...I don't know what you mean.'

'No? I think you must have misinterpreted my offer,

Beth, though I'd be lying if I said the idea didn't have a certain appeal.' He leaned forward, drawing her towards him. 'I want you, Beth. I think you want me.'

'No! You're wrong,' she protested weakly. 'Please, don't do this. It isn't fair.' The only thing she did know for sure was that she had to put a stop to this now, while there was still time. She turned away, but his hands gripped her shoulders, forcing her to look at him.

'Why deny it, Beth? Shall I prove it to you?' he muttered harshly.

'No!' She dragged her mouth away from the delicious torment he was inflicting. She shivered as his hands stroked her arms, shifting to glide down the sensitive curve of her spine.

She moaned as his mouth came down on hers, making teasing advances against her cheek, to the hollow of her throat and back to her lips. Her treacherous body arched towards him. 'Sam, this isn't fair.' Her body quivered beneath the onslaught.

'I need you, Beth,' he said thickly. His hands ran gently through her hair, moved to her shoulders, followed the curve of her breasts. A sigh trembled on her soft, parted lips.

'Tell me now that you don't want me,' he rasped. 'You can't because you know it's not true. You want me as much as I want you. You're only fooling yourself if you think otherwise.'

It wasn't true. She didn't want it to be true. She shook her head, pushing weakly against him.

'You can lie to yourself, Beth, but not to me. No one could respond as you do in my arms and not feel something. Look, you're trembling now.'

'That's because I…I don't want you to touch me.'

'You're a liar, Beth. You can't run away for ever.

Sooner or later you're going to have to let go—let the past go. Start living again. All you have to do is find the courage—take the first step.'

'I can't. Don't you see?' Her fingers dug into the soft fabric of Sam's shirt, feeling the powerful tension of the muscles beneath. Yes, he was right. She wanted him, wanted his fierce male strength as a bulwark against life itself. But she was afraid to let go, afraid to love.

Love. The realisation shocked her. How could this be love? It bore no relation to what she had felt for Tim. Sam had come into her life when she'd still been vulnerable, that was all. He had made her aware of emotions she had never experienced before, not even with Tim. But he hadn't said he loved her. Wanted her, yes. But love…that was something he reserved only for Tess.

'What is it, Beth? What's wrong? Was your marriage so special that you don't want to make room for anyone else? You're afraid I might try to usurp your husband's place. Is that it?'

'No. You don't understand.'

'But I'm trying to.' A brief hardness flared in his eyes. 'Talk to me, Beth. Tell me about it.'

'There's nothing to tell.'

'What happened Beth?'

She tried to pull away again, but his grip merely tightened. She thought about fighting him and knew it would be futile.

'We were both medical students,' she said hesitantly. 'Tim qualified about a year ahead of me. He was good company. We shared the same interests, had the same circle of friends. I suppose we more or less drifted into a relationship. You know the sort of thing—meeting at lectures, having the occasional meal or drink together.'

'What went wrong?'

She stiffened as his persistent probing began to stir more deeply, memories she had imagined were safely buried.

'I'm not sure. Possibly we grew up. I don't know.' She paused as words momentarily failed her. 'Things were fine as long as we were just friends. It was after we married that things seemed to change. He became...proprietorial. It...it was a while before I began to realise what was happening.'

She pushed back a wisp of hair and realised that her hand was shaking. 'Tim was obsessively jealous. It seemed to start so insidiously, an odd remark if I happened to meet a friend when we were together.' She gave a short laugh. 'At first I even felt vaguely flattered that he should feel jealous, as if, in some way, it was a kind of measure of the way he cared. Until, gradually, I began to realise that my friends were gradually being pushed away, and then it began to happen with my family, too.'

'Go on,' Sam said softly.

'It was Christmas,' she reflected, 'when it all seemed to come to a head, and I knew...' She drew a deep breath. 'I knew it was all over. I telephoned my mother and...and suddenly I could hear myself making excuses, explaining why we couldn't make it to a family party. I could hear her disappointment, then she said, "But we hardly ever see you these days. Is it something we've done?"' Beth looked at Sam. 'That's when I knew it had to stop. I thought when we had Sophie that he would feel more secure, but it didn't happen. If anything, things got worse.'

She looked at Sam, sensing an inner anger as he muttered something beneath his breath. Her fingers clenched.

'Did you love him?'

'I suppose I must have done. At least, I thought so at the time.' A slight shiver ran through her, though it had nothing to do with feeling cold. 'Obviously I was mistaken.'

Gentle fingers lifted her chin and began to trace the outline of her mouth. 'It wasn't your fault, Beth. You can't spend the rest of your life blaming yourself for what happened. Sometimes we just have to learn to let go.'

'I know that.' She was beginning to lose control beneath the feather-light touch of his fingers against her cheek.

'What happened?' he asked softly.

She shrugged. 'There was an argument. I was ready to go out. Sophie and I had planned a shopping trip. I'd put Sophie in her car seat and was about to leave when Tim…' She moistened her dry lips with her tongue. 'Tim suddenly accused me of going to meet someone else. I told him it was untrue, that it was ridiculous, but that only seemed to make him worse. He pushed me out of the way. I fell, and before I could get to my feet he'd driven away.'

Her voice seemed to be stuck somewhere in her throat. 'The police found him an hour later. The car had crashed. Tim died later in hospital. Sophie was badly injured. That was what hurt so much, that he could risk her life.' She dabbed at her eyes with her fingers and Sam produced a handkerchief from his jacket pocket.

She stood very still, her eyes closed, afraid that he

might see what was happening to her. She'd imagined she'd loved Tim. It was only now that she was beginning to realise that her feelings bore no relation to what she was feeling for this man.

She tensed with the need to resist the powerful feelings he was evoking. What had happened to all her resolutions not to get involved?

She sniffed quietly. 'I'm sorry I cried all over you.'

'Forget it,' he said. 'Call it delayed shock.'

She stared down at the handkerchief held tightly in her fist. 'Maybe you're right.' She managed a slight smile. 'I didn't realise how much tension I'd been storing up. It was like a nightmare when Tim died. I felt guilty, but I couldn't cry.'

'But now you know that the reason for that guilt doesn't exist, except inside your head.'

'Yes, I can see that now.' She looked at him, her eyes shining brightly. 'It's late. I really must go,' she said huskily. 'But thank you for listening. I just need some time to think things through. Do you understand?'

'Yes, of course I understand.'

She let out a slow, tremulous breath. Suddenly she knew she couldn't leave things as they were. She had kept her emotions in cold storage for so long, imagining they were safe. What she hadn't counted on was someone like Sam coming along to push aside all the mental barriers she had spent so much time carefully erecting.

'Look, I'd like to repay you for your kindness in inviting me to your party, and for listening to me. It's just an idea, but why don't you come over for supper tomorrow evening? I could cook some steaks or pasta.

I think I might even have a bottle of wine. We could talk…'

'It's a nice idea, Beth, but I'm afraid I can't.'

'I see,' she said flatly, feeling the warm colour darken her cheeks as she looked at him. With an effort she managed to force a smile. 'Well, never mind. Some other time maybe.' She shrugged herself into her jacket and was fumbling with the doorhandle when his voice stopped her.

'I appreciate the offer, Beth, but I'm going to be away for a few days. I'm sorry it's going to cause some inconvenience, but I've arranged for John to cover for me on Monday.'

She was conscious of a sudden feeling of tightness in her throat. 'Yes, I see. Well, not to worry. I'm sure we'll cope.' She took a deep breath and managed a smile. 'Something important, is it? Or just a few days' sightseeing?'

A spasm flickered briefly across his features. 'I'm meeting Tess. There are a few things we need to discuss.'

Tess. Yes, of course. How could she have forgotten Tess? The girl he had planned to marry. Beth was shocked to discover that she actually felt jealous of a girl she didn't even know.

'Well, have a good time,' she said dully. 'I'll see you when you get back.'

Twenty minutes later she let herself into the cottage and shut the door behind her. She felt incredibly tired, and more cold than she had for a very long time. Somehow she didn't think her state of mind had anything to do with memories of Tim.

CHAPTER EIGHT

IT WAS a bright, chill day when Beth drove to the practice a few days later. As she walked from the car park to the surgery flurries of dead leaves blew against her feet, swirling away to gather in sheltered corners.

She had slept badly and consequently, when she had finally drifted off, had slept so deeply that she hadn't stirred until the postman had rattled the letter-box as he'd delivered the morning mail.

Her head ached and the sight of a full waiting room was the last thing she needed right now.

Pausing at the desk to pick up the patients' case notes, she flicked through the appointments diary and frowned.

'Maggie, I don't see an appointment for Mr Lewis.'

'Lewis.' Maggie frowned. 'The name doesn't ring a bell. Is he supposed to come in?'

'Yes, he is. I want to check his blood sugar levels. I'm not convinced he's sticking to the diet I gave him, and I need to make him understand the importance of getting it sorted out.'

'I can phone him for you if you like.' Debbie glanced at Beth.

'Would you? We shouldn't have to chase the man. You'd think he'd want to get his treatment sorted out.' She raked a hand through her hair, missing the look that passed between the two women. 'See if you can get him to come in within the next few days, even if it means we have to juggle round one or two other appointments.' She shook her head. 'Does he tend to come in on a particular day?'

Maggie flipped through the pages of the diary. 'Mmm, yes—Friday.'

'Oh, well, leave it another twenty-four hours but if he doesn't call in then…'

'Don't worry. I'll get onto it.' Debbie scribbled a note.

'Oh, by the way, there's a message for you.' Maggie handed Beth a piece of paper, her face suddenly solemn. 'It's about Edie Watkins. It's not good news, is it?'

Beth read the few words, sighed and shook her head. 'No, I'm afraid not. I thought she was getting better but it seems she's had a second heart attack.' She thought about Sam. 'Any other messages?'

Maggie checked and smiled. 'No, that's your lot. But the day is young, as they say.'

No news of when Sam was expected back, then. Beth hadn't realised quite how desperately she had missed talking to him, and was unprepared for the surge of disappointment that swept over her.

Then common sense set in. He was busy, spending his days—and probably nights—with Tess. The thought that their one-time love might have been rekindled made her stomach turn over in painful spasms.

Better concentrate on other things and keep busy. Which wasn't hard to do. Surgeries were always busy at this time of year, especially in the run up to Christmas.

'I'll make a start, then.' She looked at the list. 'See if I can work my way through this lot before lunchtime.'

All in all, the morning passed remarkably quickly.

Most of the patients seemed to be suffering from coughs, colds and backache. There was also a fungal infection, a slipped disc and a little light relief when Beth was able to confirm a pregnancy.

'You're not serious?' Sally Dixon was forty years old, fairly recently married for a second time, and already had two strapping sons of seventeen and fifteen. 'Are you sure?'

Beth laughed as she washed her hands and returned to sit at the desk. 'As sure as I can be—and I have had a certain amount of practice at this sort of thing. I'd say you're about twelve weeks.'

'Well! Wow!' The woman sat back in her chair, her face suddenly flushed, her eyes bright. 'I can't believe it. And to think I'd been putting it down to a spot of indigestion.'

'It's an easy mistake to make. Indigestion, or heartburn, is one of the classic symptoms.' Beth glanced at the computer screen. 'I take it you're pleased? I see you already have two children. There's going to be quite a gap between this one and the others, isn't there?'

'I think I'll have to let you know when I've had a chance to take it in.' Sally Dixon eyed Beth with amusement. 'Yes, I am really. It's just come as a bit of a shock, that's all. I mean, I hadn't even thought...'

'I see you remarried a couple of years ago.'

'That's right. The boys and I had been on our own for about five years.'

'I take it your husband will be pleased about the baby?'

'Matt? He'll be tickled pink, once he's got over the shock.' She chuckled. 'I might have to pour him a large drink before I break the news, mind.'

Beth grinned. 'I gather the baby wasn't planned?'

'No way.' The woman blushed slightly. 'To tell you the truth, we didn't think about…well, you know. I mean, at our ages we didn't really think it would happen. I suppose we got a bit careless.' Her expression became one of concern. 'It'll be all right, though, won't it? The baby, I mean. Only I've heard there can be risks.'

'Obviously there are certain concerns when an older woman becomes pregnant. The possibility of Down's syndrome is increased, for instance. But there are tests we can do.' Beth smiled. 'As your doctor, obviously I have to discuss those risks with you. Look…' She completed her notes. 'Let's start by getting you booked in for your monthly antenatal clinic. You'll need to see the consultant at the hospital, and you'll have a routine scan, usually at about eighteen weeks. By the way, do you smoke?'

'No. I gave up about two years ago.'

'Good, because medical evidence seems to support the theory that women who smoke have smaller babies, and there's a heightened risk of cot death. Still, I can see I'm preaching to the converted. So, if you'd like to see the nurse and book your first antenatal appointment, I'll see you in a month's time, or before if you have any worries.'

Having sorted out her desk after the morning's list was completed, Beth straightened up, easing the tension in her muscles before reaching for her jacket.

She was looking forward to snatching a cup of coffee when a knock at the door drew her attention and she looked up to see Sam standing there.

'Can you spare a minute?'

'You're back!' she said, a swift wave of pleasure

hitting her at the sight of him. Then the obviousness of the statement left her feeling foolish. 'Yes—I've just finished. Come in.'

'I gather it's been a busy morning. '

'Oh, you know what it's like, especially at this time of the year. The world catches cold.'

'You seem to have coped.'

'Of course.' She shrugged herself into her jacket and dropped her mobile phone into her pocket. 'How was the trip?'

'Fine. Productive. And it was good to see London again, if only briefly.'

'And Tess? How is she?' Beth managed to keep her voice level as she said this, and congratulated herself for not letting her tension show. 'It must have been nice to spend some time together. I expect you had a lot of catching up to do.'

Sam's mouth moved in a slow smile. 'It's surprising how much you can pack into a couple of days. We managed to do some sightseeing—and some shopping, of course.'

'Of course. Well, I'm glad to hear you had such a good time. I expect you'll want to do it more often.' She tried to sound as if she meant it but wasn't sure she had succeeded when his eyes darkened and fixed on her searchingly. She looked away quickly and reached for her briefcase, then suddenly remembered. 'Oh, you wanted to see me about something.'

'I was wondering how your father is.'

She relaxed, feeling that she was on safer ground. 'He's much better. In fact, we're expecting him home in a couple of days.'

'That's great news.'

'Yes. Mum's delighted, of course. Oh, and you'll be

pleased to hear that my childminder has returned to the fold. Better still, she found me a part-time nanny who'll cover for me when I'm on emergency call at night. Her niece, who's a qualified nursery nurse, has been working in the States for the past couple of years. Now she's back and, well, she and Sophie get on like a house on fire. So, for the moment at least, everything seems to be just fine.'

'So why were you looking so serious when I walked in?'

'Was I?' She frowned. 'I didn't realise.'

'Is something bothering you?'

Apart from the fact that she only had to reach out to touch him? she thought wildly. She sighed. 'It's not a problem, not really. Edie Watkins had a second heart attack. She seemed to be doing so well, and her husband was looking forward to having her home again. I was just feeling a little depressed, that's all.'

'I'm sorry. It doesn't get any easier, does it?'

'Not for me it doesn't, anyway.' She looked at him and almost wished she hadn't as her eyes encountered his mouth, firm and attractive. His presence was far too comforting. He was solid and very real, and suddenly she was very glad he was there.

She thought of the moments she had spent in his arms, the way he had held her tight, and wished he would hold her now.

Her wandering thoughts brought heat to her cheeks, and she stirred wearily. 'I'd better make a move.'

'You're off duty this coming weekend, aren't you?'

'What? Oh, yes. I can't say I'll be sorry.'

Sam produced his car keys from his pocket and half turned towards the door. 'I was wondering whether you'd like to go for a walk, along the coastal path maybe? Weather permitting, of course. Unless you've something else arranged...'

'No.' Beth's heart gave a tiny, unaccustomed jerk. 'It sounds like a lovely idea. You...you haven't forgotten that I'll have Sophie?'

'On the contrary. I was very much hoping she'd want to come along.'

She laughed. 'I doubt if you could keep her away.'

'Great. I'll call for you. We could stop somewhere for a cream tea if you like.'

She did like. Very much!

Sophie did, too. She was waiting excitedly, coat, gloves and boots on, peering out of the window for Sam's car to arrive.

'Mummy! Mummy! He's here. Sam's here. Come on, let's go.'

Beth hurried to open the door, with Sophie beside her.

'I've been waiting for ages,' the five-year-old announced. 'Are we going to the beach?'

'No, Sophie, not today. Sorry about that.' Beth smiled at Sam.

'No, I'm sorry. I'm late. I had to make a call first.'

'Don't worry about it. I think you've made a friend for life. Sophie's had her coat on for the past hour. Look, come in while I get my gloves.'

Sam was casually dressed in denim jeans and a thick sweater beneath a leather jacket, and Beth was glad she had chosen to wear something similar, topping black ski pants with a soft, brushed shirt beneath an Arran sweater.

They made their way along the coastal path, with Sophie running excitedly ahead of them. It was a bright, crisp day. Down in the harbour below the sea was a cold, pewter grey and the sky was clear with a hint of frost to come. In a couple of hours it would be dark.

'Don't go too far away, Sophie,' Beth called, and Sam stood beside her, watching, too, a smile curving his lips.

'You're cold and your nose is red.' He put his arm round her, drawing her close to him, and she pressed her cheek into his coat, letting his warm, solid frame protect her from the wind.

'Mmm. That's nice.'

'Are you too cold? Maybe this wasn't such a good idea. Do you want to go back to the car?'

'Oh, no!' What she wanted was for this moment to go on for ever. 'I love it here. It's perfect. I hadn't realised quite how beautiful the view would be from up here. Besides, Sophie's having a wonderful time.' She tilted her head to look at him. 'It's been a lovely afternoon, hasn't it?'

'Yes, it has. Perfect.'

He held her close and she rested her head on his shoulder. For the first time in a long time she felt truly secure and at peace. But, of course, it couldn't last.

'It's getting late. Perhaps we should head back to-wards the car,' he said reluctantly. 'It'll be dark soon. Besides, I did promise you both a cream tea.'

True to his word, Sam took them to a small teashop, where they sat in front of a blazing log fire, drinking tea and eating hot toasted crumpets while Sophie tucked into a large sticky iced bun.

They were the only customers. Beth's gaze darted to Sam. He looked happy and relaxed. She found herself wondering whether he had done this with Tess, and supposed he must have. A big black cloud which she vaguely recognised as depression seemed suddenly to be sitting just above her head. She did her best to disperse it, watching as Sam made laughing attempts to steal the remains of Sophie's iced bun.

'You don't imagine she's going to give it up without a fight?' Beth grinned. 'Honestly, the pair of you are behaving like five-year-olds.'

'But I *am* five,' Sophie protested, squealing with delight as Sam made a playful grab for her glass of juice.

'Of course you are, poppet.' He kissed the top of her chestnut curls and she held out the glass to him.

Watching, Beth felt a powerful surge of affection welling up inside her. He was a good man, gentle and caring in a way that Tim, she realised now, had never been.

The thought made her throat ache and brought a strangely hollow feeling to her stomach. Suddenly she was filled with self-doubt. Sam was right, she could see that now. But she had already made one mistake. Maybe she could no longer rely on her instincts.

A smile fleetingly touched her lips. There seemed no defence against this man who had forced her to see that she *could* love again.

The smile faded as the owner of the teashop came to ask if they would like more tea and jerked her attention back to the present.

Beth's cup rattled noisily into the saucer, warmth flooding her cheeks, and she turned away quickly, aware of Sam's sidelong glance.

There was no point—no point at all—thinking that way, she silently berated herself. It was sheer folly. Sam liked her, that much was obvious. He found her physically attractive, enjoyed her company and made no secret of the fact that he wanted to be her lover.

But there was nothing more to it than that. How could there be, now that Tess had walked back into his life? He had loved her and lost her once. It wasn't likely that he was going to risk losing her for a second time, was it?

CHAPTER NINE

DECEMBER arrived on a cold, wet note. Inevitably the practice was busy and Beth found herself quietly envying Doug who was counting the days to his retirement and the move to sunnier climes.

Maureen Davies wanted some warmer weather, too. Sixty years old, she looked tired and pale and was having difficulty breathing as she lowered herself slowly into the chair.

'I really don't understand it, Doctor,' she said huskily. 'I had a cough a few weeks ago, but it seemed to clear up, and now it's back again with a vengeance and I feel awful.'

'Yes, I must admit, you don't look at all well.' Beth reached for her stethoscope. 'You say you had a cough a couple of weeks ago. Can you remember how long ago exactly?'

Maureen pressed a hand to her chest and drew a long wheezing breath. 'I suppose it must have been about three...four weeks.'

'And you say it seemed to clear.'

'Well, I thought it had. I was fine for about a week and was congratulating myself on having got over it when suddenly it started all over again, only worse.' She coughed, a deep, rattly sound. 'I can't remember when I last felt so ill, Doctor. I'm not one for coming to the surgery if I can avoid it.'

'No, I can see that.' Beth glanced at the patient's

previous medical history on the computer screen. 'You haven't actually seen a doctor for a couple of years.'

'I'm not much of a one for taking pills if I can help it. I'll take a painkiller if I have to, but that's about it.'

Beth gave a wry smile. 'I can't say I blame you. But let me just listen to your chest and see if we can find out what's going on in there.'

She made a brief but thorough examination before returning to sit at her desk. 'I'm afraid you have bronchitis, which would certainly explain why you feel so ill. It usually starts with a cold virus that spreads to the airways, and a secondary bacterial infection is quite common. You don't smoke, do you?'

'No, I never have.'

'That's good. I'm going to give you a course of antibiotics. It's important that you finish the course.' Smiling, Beth handed the woman a prescription. 'See how you get on with the tablets. Hopefully, within a few days you'll start to feel better. You might find it helpful to increase the air moisture at home. Try taking frequent hot showers—or maybe use a cool-mist humidifier by your bed.'

She rose to her feet and Maureen Davies followed suit. 'Basically, be sensible. Try to rest and drink plenty of fluids. Take paracetamol if you feel they help.'

Maureen pulled a face. 'Sounds fun, doesn't it?'

'I know, but it won't be for long. If you don't feel better after a few days, or you're at all worried, come and see me again.'

Beth watched her leave the room.

All in all, it was a busy morning. Two hours later she had seen her last patient and cleared her desk before making her way to the office.

She was sorting through some paperwork when John walked in, carrying a cup of coffee.

'Hi. I thought perhaps you could use this.'

She took the proffered cup. 'Oh, bless you. How did you guess?'

'Experience.' He grinned. 'Busy morning?'

'You could say that. I thought I'd try and get rid of some of this stuff.' She riffled through the bundle of papers. 'Where on earth does it all come from?'

'Better not ask. I've discovered that filing it in the nearest waste-paper bin works for me.'

'You're incorrigible.'

He chuckled. 'I know, but lovely with it. Oh, by the way, you do know about the PCT meeting, don't you?'

Beth glanced up, from the letter she had been reading. 'PCT?'

'Primary Care Trust?'

'Oh, Lord, yes. Sorry. Of course I've heard of it, but—a meeting?'

'Next week. It's nothing too formal. It's just that we stopped being single fundholders a few months ago, and joined forces with other practices to form a PCT. We meet occasionally to discuss joint funding for community health services, and things like how patients can be given better access to health services in their area—dentists, opticians, that sort of thing. As I said, it's fairly informal. Someone gives a talk, we ask relevant questions, then we have a drink and nibbles afterwards.'

'It sounds like a good idea. I must confess, I don't know a great deal about PCTs.'

'I think you'll find it useful. Look, tell you what, why don't we get together one evening—have a chat

and see if there are any questions we might like to ask?
What about tomorrow evening?'

'Yes— Oh, no. I promised to take Sophie to see
Disney film.'

'No problem. The evening after that, then?'

She smiled. 'Yes, I'd love to.'

'That's settled, then.' He looked at his watch. 'And
now I suppose one of us had better go and earn a crust.'

Beth playfully aimed a journal at him as he headed
for the door. She liked John. She felt at ease with him.
Which was more than could be said for the way she
felt with Sam.

She was signing letters and putting them neatly into
a folder when there was a knock at the door and
Maggie came in. She looked worried.

'Oh, Beth, I'm glad I caught you.'

'Is something wrong?'

'It's… Look, I'm sorry. Your mum just phoned.
Your dad isn't feeling too well. I think she's quite worried about him.'

Her face draining of colour, Beth was already heading for the door before the girl had finished speaking.
'I'll go straight over there. Cancel my appointments for
this evening, will you? Or ask John if he would mind
covering for me.'

In the corridor she almost collided with Sam as the
door of the room opposite opened. Other than in passing she hadn't seen him for a few days and she was
unprepared as an indefinable sense of longing surged
through her.

'Sam! I didn't know you were still here.'

'I was just trying to sort out my diary.' He looked
at her and frowned. 'Something's wrong. What's happened?'

'It's Dad.'

'Paul?'

'Mum just phoned,' Beth said shakily. 'It seems he's not feeling too well. I'm just on my way over there.'

'Did she say what's wrong?'

'No, but she must have good reason to be worried. Mum isn't the sort who panics easily.' She bit at her lower lip. 'He hasn't been out of hospital very long.' She looked at him. 'I don't suppose…'

'I'm coming with you—let me just grab my bag. We can take your car. Mine needs petrol.'

The drive to her parents' house took barely ten minutes. As they came to a halt on the drive, the door was already open and Anne came to meet them.

'Beth. Oh, and Sam. I'm so glad you got here so quickly. I didn't know what to do.'

'How is he, Mum?'

'At the moment, cross! He says I'd no business worrying you, that it's wasting your time.'

'Well, let's hope he's right. Where is he?'

'In the sitting room. I thought about trying to persuade him to go upstairs to bed, and then decided it might be best not to move him.'

Sam didn't waste any time. He headed straight for the sitting room. Beth followed blindly, mentally steeling herself for what she might find.

Paul was sitting in a chair, his eyes closed as he rested his head back against a cushion. He looked pale and his skin was clammy.

'Dad?' She moved towards him. 'How are you feeling?'

His eyelids fluttered open and he managed a smile. 'Beth, my dear. I'm so sorry. I didn't want your mother to bother you. I feel so stupid.'

'She did the right thing.' Beth knelt beside him. 'How long have you been feeling like this?'

He shook his head. 'Not long. Couple of hours or so.'

Sam was a man of speedy reflexes. The reassuring smile was an added bonus, Beth thought as with calm, unhurried movements he knelt beside her father to begin making a gentle examination.

'Any pain anywhere, Paul? Discomfort?'

The older man's hand moved vaguely in the direction of his chest. 'Some. More like pressure than pain. Not bad. Just a bit of a nuisance.' He coughed.

Sam reached for his stethoscope, applying it to Paul's chest. 'How's the breathing?'

'Bit wheezy. Not been right for a couple of days. Probably caught a cold.'

'Paul, why on earth didn't you tell me?' Beth's mother chided as she reached for his hand.

'Because I didn't want you worrying. You know I can't abide fuss.'

Beth saw Sam's lips tighten fractionally as he concentrated on his examination. A few seconds later he straightened up. 'Why didn't you call the surgery, Paul? Or at least let Beth know? One of us would have come out to see you. It doesn't have to be an emergency, you know.'

'I didn't want to be any trouble, that's all. Thought I'd get over it.'

'You have a temperature.'

'Yes, I thought so.'

'Any pains anywhere—your arms, chest?'

'Are you asking me in the most tactful way if I'm having a heart attack?'

Sam glanced at Anne. Tears glistened faintly behind

the woman's lashes as she said briskly, 'You're impossible, Paul Frazer.'

'So I've been told.' Smiling slightly, he reached out for her hand. 'I'm nothing but a worry to you, aren't I?'

Sam drew up a chair and sat down. 'Well, I can put your mind at rest straight away by saying that you're *not* having a heart attack.'

Beth gave a silent sigh of relief. 'I suspect you've been overdoing things.'

'I keep telling him he should remember he's not long been out of hospital,' Anne said. 'He never was one for taking advice. Always stubborn.'

Sam coiled the stethoscope, dropping it into his briefcase. 'You've got a bit of a chest infection. It isn't too bad, but you were right to call. I'll give you some antibiotics. I'm sure you'll find they do the trick, and you should soon be feeling a whole lot better.'

He wrote out a prescription, placing it on the nearby table. 'You're going to have to try and be more sensible, Paul. Take things more easily for a while. Gentle exercise is one thing, but I gather you've been trying to do too much too soon.' Sam's mouth firmed. 'I mean it, Paul. You're not doing yourself any favours, and it isn't fair to Anne. So ease up. You don't have to prove anything to anyone.'

'That's exactly what I tell him.'

'You're a bully, Anne Frazer.' Paul smiled and patted his wife's hand. She fumbled for her hanky and sniffed hard.

'Yes, well, someone's got to make you see sense, old man.'

It was only later, when she found herself being ushered to the car, that Beth realised she had been relieved

of her keys and was sitting in the passenger seat while
Sam drove. She was happy to let him take charge.
Right now she felt too cold and weary to concentrate.

He brought the car to a halt, and she sat gazing out
of the window, only then noticing that they were at
Sam's home, not at the cottage. But she realised it
made sense as he had left his own car behind at the
surgery.

'I don't know about you,' he said, 'but I could use
a strong coffee. Come on, it won't take long. You can
warm yourself in front of the fire. It's not far off freezing out here.'

Put like that, how could she refuse?

She followed him into the house and through to the
kitchen where Sam flipped the switch on the electric
percolator before reaching for mugs from the shelf.

'I can manage here. Why don't you go and make
yourself comfortable? You might even find a brandy.'

She gave a slight smile. 'Nice thought, but I'd better
not. I'm driving and I'm still officially on duty.'

Left to her own devices, Beth wandered through to
the sitting room. A fire had burned low in the hearth
but still gave out a comforting warmth.

Without thinking, she reached for a log from the
nearby box, dropping it into the embers. Within seconds the fire crackled into life. She stood watching the
flames, orange and blue, licking round the wood, casting a brightness into the growing gloom of a winter
afternoon.

There was something very comforting, almost hyp-
notic about a real fire. She felt safe here. There was a
strange feeling of having come home. Except, she reminded herself dully, this could never be home. For
Tess, maybe.

'Sorry about that. I was hunting for biscuits but there don't seem to be any.'

She looked up to see Sam standing in the doorway. He was studying her so intently that she wondered just how long he had been there, watching her. She ran a hand awkwardly through her hair. There was something disturbingly arousing about him as he stood with the hall light behind him, his eyes appearing a deeper blue than ever.

'Do you need any help?'

'I don't think so. Coffee's just about ready. Everything's under control.'

Except my heart, Beth thought wildly. The effect of the lamplight and his nearness were creating an intensity of sexual awareness that took her breath away.

She gave a slight laugh. 'I feel guilty. I could quite get used to being waited on.'

'Well, why not? It's been quite a day, one way or another.' He looked at her searchingly. 'You must have been worried sick. Come here,' he said softly, holding out his arms to her. 'You look exhausted.'

'It's certainly not the sort of day I'd care to repeat too often,' she murmured, but she went anyway, allowing him to enfold her in his arms, his hand gently soothing against her hair, easing away the tensions of the day.

It felt so good, so right. As if this was where she belonged. She raised her head slowly to look at him, and he groaned softly and then, suddenly, he was kissing her, his mouth making gentle, teasing advances against her lips and her throat and back to her shamelessly unresisting mouth, claiming it with a determination that left them both breathless.

She responded with a ferocity that matched his own,

driven by a raw kind of hunger. Sam drew back briefly, breathing hard as he looked at her.

'I've wanted to do that for so long,' he said huskily against her hair. 'When I'm not with you I tell myself I'll be patient, I won't rush things. But I only have to see you and all my good intentions fly out of the window. Even today, when I was worried about Paul, and I knew what you were going through, I just wanted to hold you.'

'I'm so glad you were with me,' she whispered. 'I was so scared. When Mum's call came through I immediately imagined the worst. I was so convinced Dad had had a heart attack, and I was afraid I'd go to pieces instead of helping.'

'You would have coped.' His hands moved over her, shaping her slenderness, caressing her warmly. His breath seemed to catch shakily in his throat. 'You've no idea what this is doing to me, having you so close. I want you, Beth. I want to make love to you.'

'I know,' she said weakly. Her senses seemed drugged as she looked up at him.

'I won't hurt you.' His fingers were at the buttons of her blouse.

She drew a shuddering breath as his hand moved to caress the soft curve of her breast. The effect of his touch was even more potent than she had ever imagined it could be.

'I don't want to rush things, Beth. I'm not sure I can stick to that.'

'I know.'

His hands were moving over her, arousing her again. Her limbs felt strangely weak as she clung to him, her fingers curving over his wide shoulders, taking the support they offered. She closed her eyes, moaning softly.

'This is completely crazy.'

'I know,' he breathed as he drew her closer still. His fingers slid her blouse over her shoulders.

Her mobile phone rang. Involuntarily she gasped.

'Leave it.'

'Sam, I can't. You know I can't. I'm on call.'

He cursed softly under his breath as she detached herself slowly from his arms to take the call.

'Yes, Dr Jardine speaking.' She pressed her fingers against Sam's marauding lips. 'Yes, and how long has he had the pain? You've tried giving him a dose of Calpol? No, I think you did the right thing, calling me. I'll be there in about…twenty minutes.' She terminated the call and struggled to rebutton her blouse. 'I have to go, Sam. It's a child—could be appendicitis.'

He gave a short, unsteady laugh. 'Wouldn't you just know it? Look, why don't we arrange something for tomorrow evening? We need to talk, Beth. Why don't I bring a bottle of wine over to your place?'

Beth shook her head as she shrugged herself into her coat. 'I promised Sophie I'd take her to see a Disney film. It's her favourite.'

'The evening after that?'

'I'm sorry, Sam. I can't.' She ran her tongue lightly over her lower lip. 'I'm having supper with John. He's going to put me in the picture about PCTs before the meeting next week. I feel I need to—'

'It's all right. You don't need to explain,' he said dismissively. 'I'll see you at the surgery over the next day or so. Besides, I said I'd help Tess with her packing. She's moving out of her flat and I said I'd give her a hand.'

Beth drew a shaky breath, sensing him moving away as if an invisible barrier had come down between them.

'Right.' She swallowed hard on the sudden tightness in her throat. 'Well, I'll see you.'

'You'd better go or you'll be late.'

His face had taken on a shuttered look, and Beth knew that, whatever they had shared, the moment had been lost.

Perhaps it was just as well, she thought unhappily. As he'd said, it had been a passing thought, and the kiss had been no more than a comforting gesture that had got out of control.

Maybe it was as well things had come to a halt when they had. From now on it was probably best if she kept out of his way, she decided as she drove away. The last thing she wanted was to be some sort of consolation prize while he sorted out his feelings for his ex-fiancée.

Things were fairly chaotic at the practice during the following week. Doug had gone off sick with severe laryngitis. John was in court for the best part of a day, waiting to give evidence in a drink-driving case in which a young man had been killed, and Sam was away for a couple of days at a medical conference.

On top of that, their usual arrangement to take on a locum had fallen through at the last minute, and Beth decided that there was nothing for it but to add Doug's patients to her own list.

If she'd imagined that Sam would be pleased with her display of initiative, she couldn't have been more wrong.

'What the devil is going on here?' he demanded tersely, coming in late one day to find her still taking a surgery which, by rights, should have been over at least an hour and a half earlier. 'Maggie tells me you've been working late practically all week.'

'We've been busy. In case you hadn't noticed, there's a flu epidemic going around. People are dropping like flies,' she told him crossly, hunting through the growing mountain of paperwork on her desk for an elusive file. And to think she had actually been missing this man!

'I'm well aware of the kind of pressures we're up against. That isn't the point. We're supposed to have a system that works perfectly well without you needing to be here every minute of the day.' His glance raked her. 'Look at yourself. You're white as a sheet and completely exhausted. And when did you last stop long enough to eat a decent meal?'

'Well, thanks a lot,' she retorted with dry sarcasm. 'You certainly know how to boost a girl's morale. As a matter of fact, I was out on call last night, and I've taken a clinic and a surgery today, so it's hardly surprising if I'm looking a little less than my best.'

'I've heard about the hours you've been putting in, covering for Doug and John. You've no business taking on that amount of extra work. It isn't fair to you and it certainly isn't fair to the patients.'

She stiffened at that. 'Are you saying that I'm not giving my best?'

'No one can function properly on practically no sleep.'

She glowered at him. 'Are you saying I'm not capable of doing my job?'

'I didn't say that,' he said evenly. 'But I am concerned that the smooth running of this place seems to have fallen apart in a matter of days. What the devil happened to the locum we'd arranged for?'

'He went down with flu.'

'Why wasn't I kept informed?'

'What was the point? What could you have done?' she queried tightly. 'It was hardly Doug's fault that he happened to be ill, and John didn't ask to be kept hanging around the court. Besides, I understood that Debbie did keep you in touch with what was going on.'

'I was told that everything was under control,' he said harshly.

'Which it was. For heaven's sake, Sam, you can hardly blame the office staff for telling you what they thought to be true. Everyone's under pressure.'

'Can't I? Well, we'll see about that.'

He stormed out of the room and headed for Reception. Beth grimaced, mentally steeling herself for the blast that would follow, and decided that her best course of action was to ring for her next patient.

He was behaving unreasonably. Maybe things weren't going so well between him and Tess. After all, their relationship had failed once before. Maybe they were finding that it wasn't quite so easy, picking up where they'd left off. She couldn't find it in her to be sorry about that.

With an effort, Beth dragged her thoughts back to her work, frowning as she glanced at her computer screen to familiarise herself with the notes on her next patient. She only hoped that the PCT meeting would prove to be more relaxing.

John was certainly at his most relaxed on the evening when it finally arrived. There was a good turnout of doctors from other practices in the district.

The proceedings began with a talk, which was followed by a lively question-and-answer session. Afterwards they all trooped out to enjoy the refreshments which had been laid out in the anteroom.

'It went rather well, didn't it?' John said, listening to the chatter going on around him and helping himself to a handful of crisps and a glass of white wine. 'It's good to get together every now and again—gives everyone a chance to share their views, air any worries.'

'Well, I certainly learned a lot,' Beth agreed. 'The last practice I worked for were only just in the process of applying to become a primary care trust. It certainly makes sense to combine funding. It must mean a better deal for the patients.'

'And I'm all for that.' John glanced at her plate. 'You're not eating. Try the sausage rolls. They're very good.'

'And very fattening.' Laughing, she patted her stomach.

John grinned, sliding a glance over her in a way that was decidedly male. 'I wouldn't have said you have anything to worry about.'

Beth was wearing a short-sleeved blouse of soft, silky fabric in a delicate rose colour that added warmth to her pale complexion. A calf-length skirt, cinched at the waist, fitted her perfectly. Seeing his expression, and recalling how attentive he'd been when they'd had supper a few nights previously, she wondered whether she had made a wise choice and sipped at her mineral water to hide her confusion.

'I think it all went very well, don't you?' Sam said, coming to stand beside Beth and subjecting her to a penetrating scrutiny. 'You're looking very flushed. Is John behaving himself?'

John laughed. 'Can you blame me if I'm not? This

is one beautiful young unattached lady—or hadn't you noticed? Or perhaps you're too busy thinking about Tess. Missing her, are you?'

'Let's not get personal and remember where you are,' Sam advised him coolly. 'It wouldn't look too good if we were seen to come to blows.'

'I dare say it's just that the evening has been a real success and everyone is relaxed,' Beth put in quickly before things could get out of hand. She could see that John wasn't amused, and from Sam's tone she wasn't entirely sure that he was joking.

'You're not driving, I hope?' Sam said. He looked at her. 'I have my car outside. I'll give you a lift home.'

'No.' Beth moistened her dry lips with her tongue. 'Thank you, but I have my own car.'

'Besides,' John intervened, 'I didn't bring my car so I've begged a lift and persuaded Beth to come back to my place for a coffee. You needn't worry. I'll make sure she gets home safely.'

Sam's glance shifted to Beth. 'In that case, I'll see you tomorrow. By the way, I'll take the antenatal clinic. I think you've done more than your share already.'

His smooth return to business matters left Beth feeling cross and resentful. For a while there she had actually allowed herself to imagine that he might be jealous. But she'd been kidding herself, she could see that now. Just as she'd been kidding herself all along. There was no future for her with Sam. They were colleagues, that was all. Their relationship was, and always would be, strictly professional. And maybe it was best that way, she thought as she watched him leave.

Sometimes she wished she had never met Sam

Armstrong, but she knew that even that wasn't true. He had walked into her life and turned it upside down. There might be no future in it, but there was no going back either.

CHAPTER TEN

SAM'S mood hadn't improved by the following day. Walking in to the surgery, the air of tension hit Beth even before she reached Reception.

'Morning, Maggie. I don't suppose you've seen this month's copy of the *BMJ*, have you?'

'Er, no... Oh, wait a minute, yes. I think—' She broke off as the phone rang. 'Damn! Sorry about this. I'm having one of those days. Do you mind if I just see what Sam wants?'

'No, that's fine. You carry on.'

'Yes, Doctor. Yes, I'm doing them now. No...' Maggie looked up, pulled a wry face and shifted the receiver away from her ear. 'Yes. Yes, I do realise you need them urgently. I'll have them on your desk in about— Right—two minutes. Oh, and by the way, Doctor, if you have this month's copy of the *BMJ*, Dr Jardine would like to borrow—'

She replaced the receiver and sighed.

'Oh, dear.' Beth put her briefcase down and glanced in the direction of Sam's door. 'Having a bad day, are we?'

'I don't know about Sam, but I certainly am.' Maggie gave a slight smile. 'I can't speak for everyone else, but I don't seem to have done a thing right since I walked in the door.'

'It's not like him.' Debbie came through from the office to flip the switch on the electric kettle.

'Just as well.' Maggie dragged the letter from the

printer and flung it into a folder. 'Otherwise he may find himself without a receptionist.'

'You need a coffee.' Debbie reached for two mugs.

'Make that three, will you? Strong and black for me,' Beth said. 'I have a feeling I'm going to need it. Anyone for aspirins?' She was looking through the diary when Sam erupted from his room.

'You wanted this, I think.' He dropped the journal on the desk in front of her, signed the letters with a flourish and pushed a pile of papers into his briefcase.

'In a hurry, are you?' Beth commented, hoping her voice sounded less shaky than she suddenly felt. 'Going away for the weekend?'

She was glad it was Saturday tomorrow, and that she wasn't on duty. She might even take Sophie to the park to feed the ducks. It had been a long week, one way and another. It would be nice to relax.

'Yes, I am, as a matter of fact,' he answered shortly.

'Somewhere nice?' She winced. The moment the words were out she wished them unsaid. She didn't want to know how he would be spending his weekend.

'I'm going up to London again to see Tess. What about you? I suppose you've made plans?'

She shook her head, wishing she hadn't asked. 'I thought I'd do as little as possible. I might even have a lie-in tomorrow. Sophie permitting, of course. Mind you, I don't give much for my chances. She's usually wide awake at the crack of dawn.'

'Had a heavy night with John, did you? I'd have thought you'd have learned by now that in this job you can't afford to burn the candle at both ends.'

His voice was edged with sarcasm and she looked at him, shocked by the cynicism in his tone.

'What makes you think I was out late?'

'Partly because I know John, and he's not one to miss an opportunity.'

Beth stiffened defensively and gave him a puzzled stare. 'What exactly are you trying to say? That I stayed out all night—with John?'

'Didn't you?' He snapped the locks on his briefcase shut. 'You weren't at the cottage when I drove past in the early hours this morning. One of my patients had a severe asthma attack so I was called out. Your car wasn't there, and I know you weren't on call.'

'I see. So you drew your own conclusions. I wasn't home so I must have spent the night with John—is that it?'

'I didn't say that.'

'You didn't *have* to say it. The implication was very clear. As a matter of fact,' she reminded him quietly, 'Sophie stayed with my mother last night. I knew I might be late getting away from the meeting, so it seemed the most sensible thing. Shortly after you left I got a call from Mum. She was worried because Sophie was restless and running a bit of a temperature, so I dropped John off at his place and went over there and decided to stay the night rather than drive home.'

Sam said nothing, just continued to sift through his papers. She looked at him curiously, doing her best to quell the small hope that he might have been just the slightest bit jealous.

'I thought John was your friend,' she said quietly. 'Don't you think you're being unfair? Why are you so annoyed with him? He's done nothing to deserve it.'

'I'm not annoyed with him.' He gathered up his diary and dropped it into his pocket. 'I ordered some books from a local store. They had to order them and promised they would be delivered within a week. They haven't arrived. It's damned inconvenient.'

So much for the small spark of hope that had flickered to life in her chest.

'Are they urgent?'

'Yes. I need them to take up to London tomorrow. I've just phoned the store and they say the books have arrived and are being packed now. I can pick them up in about an hour, and with any luck I can still leave here this afternoon and be in London before dark.'

'You're obviously anxious to get away. You must be looking forward to seeing Tess again.'

He reached for his mobile phone and dropped it into his pocket. 'I'd originally planned to travel tomorrow. Tess thought it might be easier to go tonight. There might be fewer delays with the traffic.'

And she'd get to spend another night with you, Beth thought. Lucky Tess. 'It makes sense, and you'll have more time together,' she said distantly. 'So, when do you expect to get back?' She cursed herself inwardly for having to ask.

'Some time on Sunday. I'm on emergency call in the evening.'

'Right, well, I'd better not delay you any longer. I'll see you on Monday, then.'

It was a long—very long—weekend for Beth. She purposely kept busy, knowing that if she relaxed even for a second she would think about Sam and Tess…enjoying being together, maybe falling in love again.

She springcleaned the cottage to within an inch of its life until Sophie grew restless and began to demand attention. Beth relented and took her to the beach where they spent an hour skimming stones at the water until a freezing wind and the first hint of a sea fog began rolling in.

By Sunday the fog had come down with a vengeance. With difficulty, Beth drove over to her parents' house where she spent the day helping to prepare and cook the Sunday lunch and making small sponge cakes with Sophie.

After tea, Anne switched on the television and minutes later came through to the warm kitchen to announce, 'The weather's getting worse. The fog's closing in and apparently they've had snow up north. They say it's causing havoc on the motorways. There's been a bad accident somewhere.'

Beth felt a small shiver run down her spine. 'Did they say where, Mum?'

'I'm not sure. I missed it, dear. I spotted an article in the newspaper and got sidetracked, so I was only half listening. I'll switch the radio on. There's bound to be something on the local news.' She listened, then said, 'Oh, it's not far from here. A few miles away.'

Beth eased Sophie off her lap and went to peer out of the window into the gathering darkness, trying to dismiss the sudden qualm that surged through her as she saw the swirling curtain of fog.

Where was Sam? Would he be home yet? He had said probably on Sunday evening. But Sam was a careful driver, and he would have anticipated the effect the sudden deterioration in the weather would have on the roads—wouldn't he?

An hour later the temperature had plummeted by several degrees and it was snowing—heavy, fluttering flakes like giant moths against the window.

She left Sophie watching a cartoon on television and

wandered into the kitchen. Maybe she should call Sam, to check up on whether he was home yet, just in case she needed to cover his emergency calls.

'Mum, I have to phone Sam to see if he's back. I may have to cover for him.'

Anne looked at her daughter, her gaze maternally perceptive. 'You're not worried about him, are you, dear? Would Sam be on that stretch of motorway?'

'I...I'm not sure.' It was the obvious route, but perhaps he would have decided to divert to the minor roads—if he'd known in time. 'I'm probably worrying for nothing. Still, I'll ring him just to be sure.'

She couldn't get rid of the tight feeling in her chest as she dialled the number, and when there was no answer to her ringing it became worse.

'He may have stopped off somewhere for a break,' Anne said.

'But he always has his mobile with him.' Beth felt her heart give a small jolt. 'I'll call John. He may have heard something.'

But John hadn't heard anything. 'Sorry, not a thing. I assumed he was back. I *hoped* he was, once I saw the weather closing in. Look, unless I hear from you to say that he's back, I'll do the emergency cover tonight. It's probably for the best anyway. I'm sure he's fine, Beth, but he'll be exhausted by the time he gets home anyway.'

'Bless you, John.'

'No problem.'

She told herself she was panicking unnecessarily, but it was small consolation. Then the phone rang and Anne came through to the kitchen. 'Beth, it's for you. It's Sam. I think he said he's on a motorway somewhere.'

Relief swamped Beth as she reached for the phone, annoyed with herself for having let her imagination run away with her.

'Sam,' she said, taking a deep, steadying breath. 'I've been trying to get hold of you. The weather's pretty awful here. I wasn't sure if you'd be back in time. Is everything all right?'

'Beth, I'm sorry it's taken so long to get through to you.' His voice was deep and gratifyingly strong. 'Look, there is a bit of a problem. I'm not going to make it back till late.'

'It's all right. John said he'll cover for you.' She hesitated. 'Sam, where exactly are you? What's wrong?'

'I'm still on the motorway. There's a lot of freezing fog, and there's been an accident. It's pretty bad. I'm going to find out what I can do to help.'

'Yes, of course.' She raked a hand shakily through her hair. 'How…how many people are injured?'

'They're still doing a count. Some of them are trapped. The emergency services are working to free them now. Look, Beth, I can't talk now. I'm needed. I'll see you later.' She thought he said something else, something which sounded like "I love you". But she told herself she must have imagined it.

He cut the call and Beth slowly replaced the receiver.

'Is something wrong?'

Beth turned to see her mother standing in the doorway, an anxious look on her face.

'There's been a pile-up on the motorway. It must have happened in the freezing fog.'

Anne dried her hands on the cloth she was holding. 'Is Sam all right?'

'I don't know. I…I think so.' Beth glanced at her watch. 'I'm going over there, Mum. I may be able to help. Will you look after Sophie?'

'Yes, of course, but, Beth, have you seen the weather out there? The fog's getting worse.'

'I know, Mum, but that's all the more reason why I have to go. It's almost dark. Things are going to get worse. They'll need all the help they can get.'

It took Beth nearly half an hour to reach the accident scene on the motorway. The police were diverting traffic, but even from a distance she could see the flashing lights of the emergency service vehicles. A car was on fire, and she could see smoke billowing from an overturned lorry. But what struck her most forcibly was the eerie silence.

'Sorry, miss, but we've closed the motorway,' the young policeman said as she brought the car to a halt and wound down the window. 'There's been a nasty accident. I doubt if we'll get it cleared until morning. You'd best divert and try to find a different route.'

'I'm a doctor.' Fumbling in her bag, she produced her identification. 'I heard about the accident and thought I might be able to help.'

'I'm afraid it's not safe down there at the moment, not until we get the fires under control. There's a lot of leaking fuel around. It could go up at any minute.'

She could smell it on the air, feel it in her nostrils, clawing at her throat.

'But there must be people still trapped in those vehicles.' She climbed out of the car to stare at the scene. 'We can't just leave them there. They might be badly injured.'

'We've got the paramedics down there, and a doctor

who was on the scene when the crash happened. He's doing a good job. Last time I saw him he was trying to help one of the trapped drivers.'

'Sam.' Beth swallowed on the sudden tightness in her throat. 'Look, I know him. We work together at the same practice. He may need help.' She reached into the car for her medical bag. '*Please*, let me go to him.'

'I'd like to, Doctor, but it isn't safe. Your friend's taking one hell of a risk as it is. I'm damn sure I wouldn't want to be within a few yards of a leaking petrol tanker. We tried to persuade him to get out of there, but he refused to leave the injured driver.'

Beth felt sick. Sam was in danger. She wanted to fight her way past them to get to him, but knew they wouldn't let her. Her hands clenched into fists as she struggled against her feelings of frustration. She looked down at the inferno and thought, I'm here, Sam. I love you. Just hang on.

'If I can't go to him,' she said at last, 'at least let me do *something*. I can't just walk away. I have extra medical supplies with me. There must be something I can do.'

'You could have a word with the paramedics at the back there.' The man waved a hand towards the men picking their way over the wreckage. 'I expect they could use an extra pair of hands.'

'Right, I'll do that. If you get a chance to talk to Dr Armstrong, will you tell him I'm here? Dr Jardine. Beth Jardine.'

Minutes later she was climbing precariously over the twisted metal debris. It was snowing more heavily now as, shining the torch ahead of her, she made her way slowly along the line of cars, checking each one to see if anyone was still trapped or injured.

For an hour she worked solidly, her breath fanning white into the freezing air as she splinted fractures, administered painkilling injections and removed glass fragments from injured limbs. Her fingers felt numb with cold, but she knew she had to keep on working and she was always aware of the acrid smell which hung in the air.

Straightening up, she eased her back.

'Doc, can you take a look here?' one of the paramedics called to her.

She clambered over a piece of crushed metal to peer over his shoulder. Even in the semi-darkness she could see that the injured man was in a bad way. His features had a bluish grey look. Her fingers automatically searched for a pulse.

'He's stopped breathing. Start mouth-to-mouth. I'll do compression.'

They worked together, the paramedic breathing gently but firmly into the man's mouth, then pausing as Beth pushed down on the breastbone several times.

'It's not working,' she said. 'We're losing him. Try again.'

They persevered until, in spite of the cold, she could feel a thin layer of sweat on her forehead. At last she felt the faint fluttering of a pulse. 'We've got him.' She almost sobbed with relief. 'Right, let's give him some oxygen.'

It was later, much later, when the last of the casualties was finally driven away in an ambulance. Beth straightened up and began to stretch her aching muscles. Her head ached and she rubbed at the back of her neck, trying to ease the build up of tension.

'They told me I'd find you here. I can't take my eyes

off you for a second, can I, without you getting into trouble?'

Gasping, she turned and saw Sam. He held out his hand to her, and with a sob she went into his arms, clinging to him, overwhelmed to see his familiar, wonderful face and to know that he was safe.

She could feel her heart thudding as he held her, his arms strong and comforting. When at last she could speak, she looked at him, feeling the weak tears well up again. She said, 'Oh, Sam, I was so scared. They wouldn't let me come to you.'

'I should think not, indeed.' He gave a short laugh which became a rasping cough. 'It was a damned tight squeeze as it was.'

'Don't joke about it, Sam.' She blinked hard. 'I suppose you do realise you risked your life down there?'

'I didn't think about it. The man was in a bad way. Someone had to help him.'

'And it had to be you,' she said crossly. She knew she was being illogical, but her mind was exhausted, shattered by the fear that she might have lost him— except that he wasn't hers to lose. She drew a deep breath. 'Is he going to be all right?'

'I hope so. It'll be a long job. He's in a pretty bad way, but I think he'll make it.' He looked down at her, and she felt the muscles in his arms tense. 'They told me you were here. You took one hell of a risk, Beth. This fog is getting thicker by the minute.'

'I had to come.' She looked up at him, her face taut with strain, to find him watching her, his lips set in a hard, fierce line. 'I was worried about you. When you phoned you said there had been an accident but you didn't say how bad it was. We heard about it on the local news. It sounded pretty bad, but it was nothing compared to what I found when I got here. Why didn't you tell me?' Her fingers moved convulsively against his jacket and she choked on a small sob. 'That tanker could have gone up in flames at any second.'

'Beth, don't.' His breathing was ragged as he held her, drawing her towards him and forcing her to look into his compelling blue eyes. 'Don't think about it. Nothing happened. Everything's fine.' His fingers caressed her hair, stroked her cheek. He was speaking softly as he held her, his own throat tightening in painful spasms. 'Don't cry, Beth. Please, don't cry.'

'But you could have been killed.' Her voice was muffled against his chest. 'I couldn't think of anything but—'

'Don't.' His lips brushed against hers, silencing the words, then he raised his head to look down at her. 'Come on, let's get out of here. Let's go home.'

They walked to her car, and he said, 'Are you all right to drive? I'm afraid my car is being towed away. It was damaged in a shunt, thankfully not too badly. I'm going to have to arrange a lease car for a while until it's repaired.'

She nodded and took Sam's arm, looking up at him. 'Come on, then. I think you've done your good deed for the day.'

The drive back to the house seemed endless. Sam sat slumped in the passenger seat, his eyes closed. She could almost feel the tension in him.

Stopping outside his house, she waited for him to move, to get out of the car—willing him not to. He drew a breath and turned his head to look at her. 'It's late. I should let you go, but I don't think I can unwind. Do you fancy a coffee?'

She nodded and followed him into the house. In the

kitchen he flipped the switch on the electric percolator and, reaching into the cupboard, produced a bottle of brandy, adding some to the coffee when it was ready. He handed a cup to her as they went through to the sitting room and she went to sit on the couch.

'I don't know about you, but I needed something a bit stronger.' He looked at her. 'The colour's coming back into your cheeks.'

He sat beside her and they gazed into the fire, feeling the heat slowly seep into their limbs as they sipped at their drinks.

'Mmm. This is good.' She turned her head to look at him and thought, Right now I want to be in your arms and I want to stay there for ever. She said, 'You'd better let me take a look at that cut.'

That was a mistake. It meant she had to move closer, into the danger zone. Her hand reached up and she was surprised to find that it was shaking.

'You were lucky. It needs cleaning but I don't think it needs stitches.' Suddenly she was angry without really knowing why. Things could have ended so differently. She could have lost him without ever having had the chance to tell him the things that really mattered. She said briskly, 'How do you feel?'

'You really want to know? Bloody awful, as a matter of fact. My head aches.'

'Well, what do you expect if you will go playing the hero?' she snapped ungraciously. 'Did you even stop to think about what you were up against out there? You were lucky, Sam. Damn lucky. Anything could have happened—' She broke off, suddenly shivering violently. Only now was she beginning to realise the full enormity of it all.

Taking several deep breaths, she half turned away,

only to feel Sam's hands on her shoulders, preventing her.

'Beth, what's wrong?'

She couldn't believe he had to ask. He might have died, and he wanted to know what was wrong.

'Nothing's wrong. What could possibly be wrong?'

His breathing was ragged as he held her, forcing her to look at him.

'Beth, it's all right. It's over.'

'But it isn't, is it?'

He continued to look at her and she averted her gaze, flustered, then, before she knew what was happening, his mouth came down on hers, relentless, firm, demanding.

They clung together, Beth offering no resistance as his hands moved over her body. He raised his head briefly to look down at her. 'I need you, Beth,' he groaned softly as his mouth made advances over her throat and eyes and then back to her mouth again, claiming it with a passion that left them both shaking and breathless.

She responded with an ardour that matched his own. This was where she wanted to be—to be part of him, to hold him, keep him safe.

'I love you, Beth.'

'I love you, too,' she said brokenly.

Sam gazed wonderingly into her eyes then, almost hesitantly, he drew her towards him again. 'I thought I was imagining things when they told me you were there,' he said. 'I'd been thinking about you, thinking what a hell of a waste it would be if—'

'No! Don't!' She pressed her fingers against his mouth. 'Don't say it, Sam. I've been such a fool, I can see that now.'

She had to force herself to speak through the tightness in her throat. 'I told myself I wouldn't let this happen again, that I would never feel this way about anyone…' Her voice broke. She looked up at him. 'I realise Tess will always be part of your life. I know how you feel about her…'

A groan rose in his throat. 'Beth, you're wrong. Yes, she'll always be special to me, but whatever there was between us was over a long time ago. I'm not even sure it ever was love. We're friends, *good* friends. But that's all there is—ever will be.'

Beth stared at him, wanting to believe him. 'But… I don't understand. She came to see you. You stayed the weekend with her. How can you…?'

'Beth, it's not the way you think,' he said softly. 'Tess is leaving for Africa next week.'

She stared at him. 'But…'

He looked at her and his hand brushed against her cheek. 'I know what people say, Beth. They think Tess broke our engagement. It's not true. It was a mutual decision. We were never really in love.'

'Sam, you don't have to—'

'I want to. I want to put the record straight.' He smiled. 'Tess and I grew up together. We spent a lot of time together and, yes, we were very close. We did become engaged. I suppose everyone took it for granted that we'd get married one day. We just sort of drifted towards it.'

He held Beth's hand and looked at her as she said hesitantly, 'But what made you change your minds?'

'I suppose we grew up. Being engaged was one thing, being married was another. I think there came a point when we both realised that it wouldn't work. We both wanted very different things. Our lives were going in different directions. I went to medical school. Tess went into teaching.'

'But…she came home.'

'Tess came back to Pengarrick to say goodbye,' he said softly.

Beth frowned. 'Goodbye? I don't—'

'She wanted to say goodbye to all her friends. Tess is going out to Africa. She met someone there when she did her year with the VSO. His name is Mark. He's out there now, setting up a school. Tess is going to join him.'

'Oh.' Beth looked at him, bemused, and he smiled.

'Tess has spent the past six months raising funds, finding sponsors. It isn't going to be a big school…' He smiled. 'Probably little more than one small classroom. But it's a start. The children will have books, paper to write on, desks, chairs. Who knows? One day maybe even a computer.'

Beth was aware of a sudden, dawning realisation. 'The books you were waiting for…they were for the school.'

'I wanted to make a contribution, to feel I'd played some small part in what Tess is trying to achieve. Can you understand that?'

'Yes. Oh, yes,' Beth said softly. 'I thought…' She turned her face up to his, her face full of anguish. 'I thought you still loved her.'

He kissed her mouth. 'I love *you*, Beth,' he said softly. 'Only you. I want to spend the rest of my life with you—and Sophie. If you think she'll have me.' His eyes glittered with quiet amusement.

'Oh, I don't think there's any doubt about that.' She sighed, nestling contentedly against him. 'You're already her hero.'

He drew her roughly towards him and kissed her until they broke apart breathlessly. 'And what about you, Beth?'

'Oh, Sam, I love you. It took me a while to admit it, even to myself. But I *do* love you. I want to spend the rest of my life with you.'

'That's going to be a long, long time, Beth.'

'I'm so happy,' she murmured softly, as she snuggled into his warm embrace. Then she remembered. 'Oh. I suppose I'd better call my parents…'

'Later, Beth,' he said huskily. 'Call them later.' He nuzzled at her cheek. 'Have I told you lately that I love you?'

'Mmm.' She sighed lazily, turning her face up to his. 'But tell me again, Sam. Just to be on the safe side.'

Modern Romance™
...seduction and
passion guaranteed

Tender Romance™
...love affairs that
last a lifetime

Medical Romance™
...medical drama on
the pulse

Historical Romance™
...rich, vivid and
passionate

Sensual Romance™
...sassy, sexy and seductive

27 new titles every month.

*With all kinds of Romance for
every kind of mood...*

MILLS & BOON®

Makes any time special™

MAT4RS

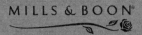

MILLS & BOON

Medical Romance™

EMERGENCY RESCUE *by Abigail Gordon*

Dr Jemima Penrose's return home is difficult enough without developing a relationship with new colleague Jack Trelawney. Jack is a lifeboat volunteer, and Jemima is all too aware of the danger that places him in. However, when faced with the possibility of losing Jack, Jemima realises he's worth risking her heart for…

THE CONSULTANT'S RECOVERY
by Gill Sanderson

When a freak accident left Jonathan Knight blinded, the charismatic consultant was determined to take control of his life. And that was where Tania Richardson came in. As she taught him to cope Jonathan found himself drawn to her. But Tania was holding back, and somehow it was all linked to his chances of recovery…

THE PREGNANT INTERN *by Carol Marinelli*

Surgeon Jeremy Foster is a carefree bachelor. Until he meets his new intern! Dr Alice Masters – six months pregnant – brings out instincts he hadn't known he possessed. Jeremy worries about her working too hard and he hates the thought of her bringing up a baby alone. But there isn't much he can do - unless he swaps the role of boss for that of husband!

On sale 3rd May 2002

GIVE US YOUR THOUGHTS

Mills & Boon® want to give you the best possible read, so we have put together this short questionnaire to understand exactly what you enjoy reading.

Please tick the box that corresponds to how appealing you find each of the following storylines.

32 Richmond Square

They're fab, fashionable – and for rent.   When the apartments in this central London location are let, the occupants find amazing things happen to their love lives. The mysterious landlord always makes sure that there's a happy ending for everyone who comes to live at number 32.

How much do you like this storyline?

❑   Strongly like   ❑ Like   ❑ Neutral – neither like nor dislike

❑   Dislike   ❑ Strongly dislike

Please give reasons for your preference:

_____

_____

The Marriage Broker

This city agency matches marriage partners for practical as well as emotional reasons. Upmarket, discreet and with an international clientele, The Marriage Broker offers a personal service to match clients' needs and situations.

How much do you like this storyline?

❑   Strongly like   ❑ Like   ❑ Neutral – neither like nor dislike

❑   Dislike   ❑ Strongly dislike

Please give reasons for your preference:

_____

_____

A Town Down Under

Meet the men of Paradise Creek, an Australian outback township, where temperatures and passions run high. These guys are rich, rugged and ripe for romance – because Paradise Creek needs eligible young women!

How much do you like this storyline?

❑ Strongly like   ❑ Like   ❑ Neutral – neither like nor dislike
❑ Dislike   ❑ Strongly dislike

Please give reasons for your preference:
_____

_____

The Marriage Treatment

Welcome to Byblis, an exclusive spa resort in the beautiful English countryside. None of the guests have ever found the one person who would make their private lives complete…until the legend of Byblis works its magic – and marriage proves to be the ultimate treatment!

How much do you like this storyline?

❑ Strongly like   ❑ Like   ❑ Neutral – neither like nor dislike
❑ Dislike   ❑ Strongly dislike

Please give reasons for your preference:
_____

_____

Name: _____

Address: _____

_____

Postcode: _____

Thank you for your help. Please return this to:

Mills & Boon (Publishers) Ltd
FREEPOST SEA 12282
RICHMOND, TW9 1BR

NO STAMP NEEDED – postage has been paid.

2FREE

books and a surprise gift!

We would like to take this opportunity to thank you for reading this Mills & Boon® book by offering you the chance to take TWO more specially selected titles from the Medical Romance™ series absolutely FREE! We're also making this offer to introduce you to the benefits of the Reader Service™—

- ★ FREE home delivery
- ★ FREE gifts and competitions
- ★ FREE monthly Newsletter
- ★ Exclusive Reader Service discount
- ★ Books available before they're in the shops

Accepting these FREE books and gift places you under no obligation to buy, you may cancel at any time, even after receiving your free shipment. Simply complete your details below and return the entire page to the address below. *You don't even need a stamp!*

YES! Please send me 2 free Medical Romance books and a surprise gift. I understand that unless you hear from me, I will receive 4 superb new titles every month for just £2.55 each, postage and packing free. I am under no obligation to purchase any books and may cancel my subscription at any time. The free books and gift will be mine to keep in any case.

M2ZEA

Ms/Mrs/Miss/Mr ....Initials...................................

BLOCK CAPITALS PLEASE

Surname ....

Address ....

....

....Postcode...............................

Send this whole page to:
UK: FREEPOST CN81, Croydon, CR9 3WZ
EIRE: PO Box 4546, Kilcock, County Kildare (stamp required)